BROTHERHOOD

Mohamed Mbougar Sarr

BROTHERHOOD

*Translated from the French
by Alexia Trigo*

Europa
editions

Europa Editions
1 Penn Plaza, Suite 6282
New York, N.Y. 10019
www.europaeditions.com
info@europaeditions.com

Copyright © Présence Africaine, 2015
Published by arrangement with Agence litteraire Astier-Pécher.
ALL RIGHTS RESERVED
First Publication 2021 by Europa Editions

Translation by Alexia Trigo
Original title: *Terre ceinte*
Translation copyright: © 2021 by Europa Editions

*This work received the French Voices Award for excellence
in publication and translation. French Voices is a program created and funded
by the French Embassy in the United States and FACE Foundation.*

Library of Congress Cataloging in Publication Data is available
ISBN 978-1-60945-672-6

Sarr, Mohamed Mbougar
Brotherhood

Book design by Emanuele Ragnisco
www.mekkanografici.com

Cover illustration taken from an image at Shutterstock

French Voices Logo designed by Serge Bloch.

Prepress by Grafica Punto Print – Rome

Printed and bound in Great Britain by Clays Ltd, Elcograf S.p.A.

CONTENTS

To Malick, my father,
to Astou Mame Sabo, my mother,
to Baba, Sëñ bi, Mara, Khadim, Souhaïbou,
Cheikh, and my entire family.
And to my Mellie.

But above all, I dedicate this novel to my grandmother Marie
Madeleine Mboyil Diouf, who passed shortly before its release.
She didn't know how to read. I would've loved to read it to her
and translate it for her into Serer.

BROTHERHOOD

PART ONE

CHAPTER 1

The crowd had been waiting since dawn and could now barely contain its excitement: it was growing impatient, whispering and whistling: soon, it would have to witness death. Abdel Karim felt it. But he decided to let the scene play out and the nervousness rise. He believed that this kind of atmosphere was necessary in order for endings to become beautiful tragedies.

The wait had begun early: just after the *Fadjir*[1] prayer, long processions of shadows formed and strange silhouettes suddenly filled the streets of Kalep, converging toward the huge City Hall square. There was something fascinating in this procession; the crowd walked, moved forward, crept up; it was imposing, irresistible, and slow, its movements resembling the maneuvers of an ancient phalanx. All of this was done in a silence only poetic in its solemnity. A silence barely disrupted by the noise of the old slippers and sandals being dragged on the laterite or the asphalt. Only occasionally, the voice of a man or a woman asked in a gentle whisper:

"At what time will it happen?"

"At ten o'clock *in Shaa Allah*,"[2] answered another voice.

Then, silence.

After a long wait, Abdel Karim had arrived in a car, followed

---

[1] First prayer of the day for Muslims, at dawn.
[2] By Allah's will.

by those in his inner circle. He was a giant. He was not wearing a turban like his men were: his face was uncovered, his bald head exposed under the intensity of the sun. He looked out at the overexcited crowd that was anxiously waiting for him to speak. He made a grand gesture with his hand, and the silence was complete. His powerful voice resonated throughout the square.

"*Audhu billahi mina-Shaitan-nir-Rajeem.*[3] By the grace of God, may my words be pure and filled with the light of truth and justice."

"Amin," whispered the crowd.

The giant continued:

"*Salamu Aleikum,*[4] People of Kalep, I salute you. May He flood each and every one of you with His Grace for having traveled here this morning. I will not be long. You know what brings me here, and it will soon be time. I simply wanted to remind you that whoever may transgress the fundamental Law of Allah, *Subhanahu Wa Ta Ala,*[5] and of His prophet *Mohamadu Rassululah . . .*"

"*Sallalahu 'Alayhi Wa Sallam,*"[6] interrupted the crowd in a deep voice.

". . . whoever may transgress the Law will be punished according to the penalty intended in the Noble Quran. I will see to it personally. I will not back down under any circumstance, and will implement the penalties of the Law, *in Shaa*

---

[3] Literally: "I seek refuge in Allah against the stoned demon." Ritual in Islam with which one often begins a speech in order to put oneself under Allah's protection.

[4] Peace be with you. A greeting or form of introduction.

[5] "Glorious and Exalted may He be." Saying used when speaking of Allah.

[6] "May the blessings and the salvation of Allah be upon him." Saying in Islam used when the Prophet Muhammad is mentioned.

Allah. Remember, people of Kalep, that the Law is the Path to Salvation. Never forget this, and let no one dare think that the critics from the West, those who consider the Law to be barbaric . . ."

"*Astaghfirullah*,"[7] whispered the crowd.

". . . let no one," he continued, "dare believe that these criticisms might be true. Those who utter such criticisms are henchmen of Sheïtan; they have no goal other than to divide us, and thus to distance us from the Lord. The only Law which we know, the only one that matters to us, is that of God. May Allah burn the sinners of the West, may Allah protect us from the Devil. May He guide us and give us the strength to pray for Him and obey Him always! May Allah make Peace reign! *Allah akbar! Allah akbar! Allah akbar!*"[8]

"*Allah akbar, Allah akbar!* Long live the Brotherhood!" yelled the crowd, transfixed.

At that moment, the armed men standing behind Abdel Karim lifted their rifles to the sky and fired. The bangs mixed with the shouting. And all of this tremendous noise from both human and mechanical voices ascended to a God who was not only being praised, but also pelted with bullets.

Abdel Karim raised his hand in a majestic fashion. The shots ceased as the voice of the crowd, exhausted, died down.

"Now, my brothers, it is time to do what we all came here for. Bring them out!"

The trunk of a car was opened, and two shapes resembling human bodies were pulled out. They were naked. There was a man. There was a woman. They were propelled forward by the force of blows to their backs and sometimes, when they showed resistance, to their kidneys or shoulder blades. Then,

---

[7] "I ask Allah for forgiveness." Saying to express repentance in Islam.
[8] "Allah is [the] greatest."

they would fall only to rise again with great difficulty. Their hands were tied behind their backs. The woman appeared exhausted; her legs gave way, and each of her steps looked as if it would be her last. At one point, she collapsed and seemed unable to move. One of the hangmen, in a moment of either pity or pragmatism, initiated a gesture to lift her up. The voice of Abdel Karim rose at once:

"The impure are not to be touched!"

The guard gave up on helping the bound woman and gave her a kick instead to redeem himself. The man, on the other hand, was trying to walk steadily, but by the way he dragged himself one could not help but sense the weariness of a body that had been subjected to the worst abuses. He was being struck roughly in the kidneys and on the neck. He fell often but always got up as quickly as he could. His courage must have irritated one of his guards, who kicked him in his bare genitals. The man fell with a bestial roar, amplified by the surrounding silence. He was only echoed by the woman's cry, which was just as heartbreaking. And that was it. The silence returned. The man was on the ground. The pain seemed excruciating. He squirmed, convulsed, and then stiffened.

"Lift him."

He was lifted up. His dusty body offered onlookers the sight of wounds still bloody. He could not stand, and fell. They brought him up to his feet anew, but like a child whose legs are still fragile, he found himself on the ground once again.

After a few attempts, he was successfully lifted from the ground, and the small group finally reached Abdel Karim.

"Here they are," said Abdel Karim, extending his hand toward the couple all while maintaining his gaze on the crowd. "Here are the adulterers who are going to receive the punishment they deserve. But first, I would like for their parents, if they are present, to come forward."

There was a movement in the crowd. Everyone turned

around, looked to the left, looked to the right; everyone wanted to see who was responsible for having brought *that* into the world. Two men and one woman finally began walking toward Abdel Karim, the two condemned, and the three executioners. Once they reached them, they came to a stop.

"*Assalamu aleïkum*, my brothers."

"*Aleïkum Salam*," the two men who had just arrived responded in harmony.

"Who are the girl's parents?"

The woman in the group came forward, followed by a man dressed in a big, long-sleeved blue caftan. The woman wept silently. The man betrayed his emotions, despite straining to maintain a dignified face.

"Are you the father?"

"Yes," answered the man.

"And you, *Adja*,[9] are you the mother?"

The woman, body convulsing in sobs, could not respond.

"She is the mother," said the man in her place.

"Well," resumed Abdel Karim, "do you have anything to say to her, before . . . ?"

At that moment, the mother could not contain herself any longer and cried out. She wanted to approach the convicted woman. Abdel Karim interrupted her:

"The impure are not to be touched."

"I am her mother," the woman groaned.

"That changes nothing."

The mother collapsed, rolled on the ground, and continued to moan. Around her, nobody reacted. Abdel Karim looked at her. The father, on the other hand, was staring at something skyward in the distance. The girl, who had not yet made a sound, fell to her knees. Both women cried.

---

[9] Form of respect addressed to respectable women of a certain age. It is also addressed to women who have made the Pilgrimage to Mecca.

"And you, El Hadj, do you have something to say?"

The man cleared his throat and spoke without looking away from the sky:

"You have disappointed me, my daughter. You have caused me great shame. You, on the other hand," he said looking for the first time at his kneeling wife. "Pick yourself up and stop behaving like a dog. All of this is your fault; you have failed to educate your daughter. Stand up!"

The woman, still in tears, remained still. She seemed exhausted. The father, overwrought, grabbed her violently and did not so much lift her from the ground as yank her from it. The mother moaned but remained standing, her head lowered, her face covered in dirt which now blended with her tears.

"*Assalamu Aleïkum*," said the father, whose eyes were also veiled with tears. Then, without waiting for a reply, he took his wife by the hand, and the two of them walked slowly back toward the crowd where they disappeared and became anonymous once again.

Abdel Karim watched them recede into the crowd without displaying any sign of emotion whatsoever. Still on the ground, the girl continued to cry.

"And you, *Aladji*,[10] are you the man's father?"

"Yes," replied the other old man.

"Where is the mother?"

"She did not come. She had no place being here. I forbade her from coming."

"Do you have anything to say to your son?"

As his answer, the old man spit violently in the direction of the condemned man. The spit reached the man's torso. Then, with a scowl of repulsion, he added:

---

[10] Modification of El-Hadj, a form of respect which is ordinarily given to respectable men of a certain age, as well as to those who have made the Pilgrimage to Mecca.

"He is no longer my son. He never was."

"*Assalamu Aleïkum*, my brother," Abdel Karim contented himself to reply.

"*Aleïkum Salam. Allah akbar*, long live the Brotherhood."

Then the father turned around and, with a proud demeanor, went back into the crowd. His son did not say a word; he had manifested no emotion, not to his father's spit, nor to his words.

"My brothers, by the Grace of God, we are now going to proceed with the punishment. May this serve as an example to all. Adultery is one of the capital sins. The Law punishes all adultery. The Brotherhood will not remain blind to any sin. May God guide us."

Abdel Karim ordered that the man be made to kneel in the same posture as the girl.

There were three executioners for two condemned. The former had to make sure that the latter would die. Next to this group stood Abdel Karim, his face drenched in sunlight. The crowd seemed dead, and yet its nerves were on edge, its breath held, anxious, excited, palpable in all of its shudders.

"Aim!" ordered the giant.

The executioners loaded and aimed.

Abdel Karim eyed the two condemned people one last time. They were both beautiful, barely twenty years old.

"Fire!"

Three shots resounded and their echoes remained suspended in the air like a cloud of dust. The young lovers had fallen without a cry. The girl had two holes in her breast. The man had received a bullet in the middle of his forehead.

They were no longer holding hands.

"*Allah Akbar!*" yelled Abdel Karim.

The crowd—immersed in the smell of both dust and death—repeated Abdel Karim's cry in chorus as though it had been one of liberation.

CHAPTER 2

A full moon and a starless sky engulfed Kalep. The city, which had been animated earlier by talk of the morning's execution, now felt empty. A few vagrants wandered aimlessly in this urban desert—sometimes alone and sometimes in groups. Occasionally, one of them would cast a few incomprehensible words into the night, words routinely interrupted by delirious laughter. These words were immediately echoed by the sympathetic cries and exclamations of other vagrants, in recognition of a shared fate. And, for a few seconds, this strange and improvised chorus rose to a litany. It was impossible to tell if it was sad, joyous, or desperate, happy or mournful. It may have been all of those things at once, and periodically it reached a kind of grace, the light, soft, captivating grace of a nocturne. Then, suddenly, it faded back into the night just as it had sprung from it; and the empire of silence reigned once again, more powerful still. In the privacy of their homes, people lost interest in this fortuitous concert. Without a word, they all carried on with their own thoughts or occupations.

"Barking dogs would have been better! My god, these lunatics are terrible singers!"

"There are no stray dogs in Kalep anymore, sis. Actually, there are no dogs in this city at all, unless the people muzzled and hid them all."

"Ah, that's true . . . I hadn't noticed. I haven't seen Pothio, the nasty neighborhood stray, in a few weeks now. You know, the one who scares me. He doesn't come around here any-more. But why not? And why aren't there any dogs?"

"We've killed them all, burned them and piled them up at the south edge of the city. You can still see the heaps of ashes and what's left of their carcasses. We killed them because we believe they're satanic animals, that they attract the Devil."

Idrissa immediately regretted speaking so crudely to his sister.

"What are heaps?"

"Piles . . ."

"Okay. But who killed them?"

"You know very well . . ."

"Them again . . . How mean! But why?"

Idrissa Camara smiled sadly at his little sister's indignation. Rokhaya was only nine years old. The frankness of her anger was both moving and ridiculous. "Yes, they are mean," he thought to himself as he looked at the child who, having already forgotten her anger and regained her usual joyous mood, ran into the arms of her mother as she entered the room. Idrissa went to the living room window, which overlooked one of the main streets of the city's center. There, he held still for a few long minutes, as if he was waiting for a miracle to happen.

He was a young, seventeen-year-old man. He was tall, slim—refined, he liked to say—and beautifully proportioned. His eyes were bright, and the contrast between their luster and his dark skin conferred an intensity to his gaze that was unusual, unflinching, and melancholic all at once.

The young man, whose eyes were fixed on the lifeless street, was stroking the few hairs which had begun to grow on his chin. Lost in thought, he was slow to notice that the street was coming to life. It wasn't until his sister began to prance around and yell: "They're here, they're here! I want to see them! Carry me, Idy!" that he awoke from his daydream.

From his window, Idrissa could see six jeeps equipped

with machine guns scouring the streets. They appeared even more frightening in the night. There were armed men sitting in the back seats of each vehicle. Their motionless silhouettes were barely discernible in the darkness. The young man's gaze hardened. The vehicles were lined up one behind the other and advancing slowly. Their machine guns were pointed toward the sky; their cannons glistened in the darkness with a virginal sheen. For a few seconds, there seemed to be some sort of duel to the death between the young man and this procession which resembled a steel anaconda, in which each jeep was one of the snake's rings. Idrissa kept his eyes on them until they disappeared, and the sound of their engines had faded into the distance. His expression then regained some humanity.

During all this time, Rokhaya had been stirring restlessly and shouting at her brother's feet, pulling him, scratching him, hitting him, even pretending to cry in the hope that he might pick her up and let her see the jeeps—which she had been the first to notice. The procession of these armed jeeps had become customary, almost a ritual: the young girl anticipated their arrival with the same excitement and wonder that children cultivate toward unusual things, those that feed their imagination. Over time, Rokhaya had learned to recognize the sound of the vehicles and to notice their headlights.

"There's nothing left to see, Rokhy. They passed by quickly."

And as Rokhaya collapsed in tears, the young man retreated to his room on the first floor after telling his mother, who had gone back to the kitchen, to call him once she had finished preparing dinner. He locked himself in his room. His sister had already stopped crying.

"Before, when I was little, I used to cry because I couldn't watch the procession of the fake lion. Today, Rokhaya is crying because she couldn't watch the armed jeeps . . ."

He thought again of the jeeps, which crawled slowly through the streets and recognized, reluctantly, that this convoy was nothing short of majestic. He immediately banished this thought from his mind and blamed himself for having had it.

"What a country . . ."

This time, Idrissa Camara had spoken softly.

CHAPTER 3

I n the kitchen, Ndey Joor Camara, born Sarr, was focused
on dinner. The familiar smell of her *cerre*[11] promised the
delight of the meal to come; it filled the house, enticed the
taste buds, aroused the palate, and sharpened the appetite.
Ndey Joor Camara was the best cook in the city and was
among the five greatest in the province. At least that was the
common consensus. Among the many benefits she received
from her strict education, the most remarkable was her mas-
tery of the art of Sumalese cuisine. By Ndey Joor Camara's
skilled hand, Sumalese cooking became gastronomy. She could
make anything: she could mix the best ingredients to produce
the most outstanding meals, which looked and smelled as wonderful as they tasted; she could extract the most delicate flavors
from unusual ingredients; she knew how to free the finest,
most subtle aromas from her dishes. Her cooking was light
without being bland, well-seasoned without being ordinary. In
addition to her culinary genius, she had an impeccable knowledge of local Sumalese produce. In other words, she knew of
the best ways to use it, to celebrate it, to sublimate it. She knew
how to cook all kinds of dishes, despite never having opened
one of those cookbooks that leave no room for the two most
important aspects of fine dining, namely creative freedom and

[11] Millet based dish, associated with fertility, often served with different
sauces and popular in Western Africa. Pronounced: cheh-reh.

improvisation. From the most traditional to the most innovative, and from the most complex to the simplest of Sumal's gastronomic repertoire. She cooked with intuition and, more importantly, with her heart: she connected with the food, exalted it constantly, played with it, with its aromas and its customs. This was reflected in her dishes; and her cooking, among the most popular in Kalep, was always full of surprises, even in the most famous and popular dishes. It carried a je ne sais quoi which always made you say, "This is Ndey Joor Camara's touch." In the same way you'd highlight an artist's singularity by referring to his or her style, voice, or technique, when speaking of this woman, her unique excellence was best described by referring to her touch.

Encouraged by her family, at one point Ndey Joor had even opened a restaurant. It became the busiest not only in the city, but in the entire province. Through word of mouth, the reputation of Ndey Joor Camara's talent had quickly spread beyond the borders of Kalep. All of her tables were reserved beginning at ten thirty for lunch, and at six for dinner, even though people usually dined two or three hours later in Kalep. But it is well known that the prospect of a big feast levels out all discretion and restraint. People came from Soro, Bantika, Akanté, from all neighboring cities of Kalep, to dine at Ndey Joor's. They waited in line, pushed each other, and sometimes even fought—this had actually happened—to have the privilege of dining at one of the sixty tables at the *Çinn-gui*.[12] To this day, all of Kalep remembers the surreal scenes of never-ending queues and huge gatherings of people in front of the restaurant's closed doors. A human tide, bustling and starving, waiting for the doors of paradise to open. If, for some reason, there

[12] The Cauldron.

was a delay, a tremendous and ghastly voice would chant: "*Yërmandé, añ vi!*"[13] There was something truly terrifying about this.

But once the doors opened! Once they opened! It was the most spectacular pushing and shoving anyone had ever seen. It looked like Hamilcar entrusting savages with his herd of elephants at the battle of Macar. Seeing the spectacle of these starving men rushing to throw themselves at those tables, Flaubert might've written "it was the seventy-two elephants charging down in a double line"[14] without cause for accusation of analogy or boldness. The same crowd which had once been unified by hunger now split, separated, and broke apart because of this very same hunger. People would push each other; and in a crowd where intelligence had temporarily withdrawn itself, suits fought against rags, company managers against modest people, and bosses against beggars. Class conflict drives History. Hunger drives class conflict.

Far from being flattered, Ndey Joor had very quickly become overwhelmed by her success. These fighting incidents terrified her, and she felt harassed: people called her constantly to make reservations, to suggest partnerships, or even contracts with big Bandiani hotels. She even received threatening anonymous letters. Her friends, in whom she confided, believed the letters came from the owners of competing restaurants who were losing their clients to the *Çinn-gui*; as for her son Idy, he believed these letters were written by the friends themselves: "Because of you, their husbands no longer eat at home," he'd tell her with a smile.

Still, after two painful months during which she had already returned her original investment and then some (some diners,

---

[13] "Lunch, for God's sake!"
[14] *Salamnbô*, Chapter VIII, (J.W. Matthews, Trans.).

when asked: "Do you want that to stay or to go?" would respond without hesitation: "Both"), Ndey Joor inflicted the worst of punishments on Kalep: she closed down her restaurant. People resented her, begged her, and offered her all kinds of deals. She refused. That is how the *Çinn-gui* closed, a restaurant that the people of Kalep will remember for generations to come.

Today there is a hardware store where the restaurant used to be. But, written in red letters on the building's foundation, one can still see a proverb that Ndey Joor Camara had chosen as her slogan: "*Çinn su maree neex su baxee xeen.*"[15] The manager of the hardware store, who used to be a regular customer at the restaurant, had kept it as a symbol of remembrance.

[15] Wolof Proverb: "A dish's aroma announces its delight."

CHAPTER 4

Once Rokyhaya was sound asleep, mother and son found themselves alone in the living room. Sitting side by side on the couch, they listened to the province's radio, which was broadcasting a religious sermon.

"What's on TV?"

"Probably the same thing that's on the radio, with the added bonus that you get to see the face of that idiot who thinks he's God."

They were silent. The voice on the radio was quoting a verse.

They weren't really listening. Or, if they were, they weren't really concentrating, catching only bits and pieces, as if something was veiling their attention. They both loved these moments in which sweet daydreaming mingled confusedly with lazy thoughts.

"Two people were executed this morning."

Idrissa said this as if it were inconsequential. His mother paused for a moment of silence before answering, with a tired voice:

"I know. The shots woke Rokhaya and she came to our room crying, seeking comfort. I was scared too, but I tried to reassure her. Your father had already left. Did you know either of them?"

"These days, we know pretty much all of those who die. Today, it was Aïda Gassama and some Lamine Kanté."

"Aïda? The daughter of El Hadj Seydou and Aïssata?"

"Yes."

"Oh, my goodness . . . *Ina lihali wa ina ilayhi wa rad-jhun*[16] . . . Wasn't she your age?"

"She was eighteen."

"And the boy?"

"Apparently, he was from Bantika, not from here. He was twenty."

Ndey Joor Camara said another prayer for the dead. Shortly after, she was struck by overwhelming fatigue.

"They will go to heaven," she sighed deeply.

"I don't know. They're dead, and that's that."

"What did they do?"

"They may have been in love. They slept together. They were caught. The night patrol. Abdel Karim came. Did you hear how the crowd yelled?"

"I heard. I heard . . . ," she repeated a few moments later. "May God help us."

"Is that the same God in whose name these people were killed? How could he possibly help us?" replied Idrissa.

Ndey Joor Camara didn't answer and closed her eyes.

The June air was heavy. Winter was coming, yet the heat that evening was unbearable. Idrissa was fanning himself slowly with a newspaper. At times he'd pay attention to the monotone voice escaping from the radio.

"*. . . our province is destined to be a peaceful province, fully devoted to serving God. By God's will, the Brotherhood is the instrument of this peace. We invite the people of Bandiani, be they from Soro, Bantika, Kalep, or any other city, to join the Brotherhood and help it serve the Law of God. We were advised to unite, we must . . .*"

---

[16] Prayer for the dead.

Idrissa turned around to face his mother. What did she think of all this? She must be scared and wondering, like everyone else and certainly like he was, how all this could have happened.

". . . in Kalep, two young adults received the ultimate punishment for their sins. They had sexual relations even though they were not married, not even engaged. Their punishment should have been a good beating. They should've been beaten a hundred times. But when confronted with their insolence and refusal to repent, the commander of Kalep's troops Abdel Karim Konaté received the order from El Hadj Majidh, Great Cadi of the Brotherhood, supreme judge of the Islamic tribunal, to proceed with an execution by fire. This was done today, by the will of God and with the utmost and purest respect for human dignity and . . ."

Idrissa found it strange that he had never spoken to his mother about what was happening. But what would they have told each other that they didn't both already know? Idrissa thought it was ultimately pointless to speak. He also knew that this thought was probably the Brotherhood's greatest victory: making people believe that communication is futile, and that the Brotherhood can speak on their behalf, and can better express their thoughts in its own language. By relieving them of their right to speak, the Brotherhood was also relieving them of their need to think. Every authoritarian regime rises in this way: it manages to convince its people of the futility of communication. The illusion of this futility, along with people's indifference toward language, becomes an individual and collective value. But this is not just a matter of the eradication of language: propaganda insidiously manages to convince those it targets that the extinction of their voice is a welcomed necessity. The people become silent because they no longer deem it necessary to speak, since everything seems clear and obvious to them. Of course, in reality, nothing is really clear. And in the face of this false clarity, ideology deafens, grows, and thrives. Idrissa knew this, but he continued to be silent. The futility had gotten the better of him and, along with it, so had the Brotherhood.

"... *and all of the other sins will be punished. This is the Will of God, always. The Brotherhood is the Future* ... *God is with us. The Brotherhood* ..."

Ndey Joor Camara, sensing the weight of her son's eyes upon her, opened her own. She grabbed his hand and smiled, as if to reassure him. The pressure of her arm, of her eyes and her smile, comforted the young man, who felt almost sorry for pulling his mother out of her daydream.

"Everything will be alright, my son."

Before even awaiting a reply, she stood up and headed toward the bathroom.

"I'm going to perform my ablutions," she said.

"I wonder how you still have the strength and courage to pray."

"More than strength and courage, I have hope."

"I no longer do."

"You have no right to give up."

"Everyone should have that right," he whispered.

On that note, he looked toward the living room door, next to which hung a framed photo of his family taken seven years earlier, on Rokhaya's second birthday. His mother, more radiant than ever, carried a crying Rokhaya with a discreet and soft smile. He recognized himself, at ten years old, sitting sideways and bearing a smile displaying two missing teeth. Next to him there were two men, also smiling, complicit in their joyous mood, perhaps even concealing some mischief. The elder of the two had his arms over the shoulders of the other, who was to his right, and who was raising his fist to the sky. His father and older brother.

But that was a different time, an earlier time. What was left today of his father and older brother?

With that question in mind, which he could not find the strength to answer, he was seized by a sort of nostalgia and suddenly felt the urge to forget all of the memories of that time. All the while, the voice on the transistor, still relentless, seemed to be finishing its speech:

"... *May God protect you from the infidels. May you sleep in peace, because the Brotherhood is protecting you, by the Will of God. And remember...*"

He stood up, turned off the device, and returned to sit on the couch. The house fell silent, and all he could hear was the gentle murmur of his mother's voice, praying.

Chapter 5

My name is Aïssata and I was there. I would have wanted you to be there, too. Yes, I would have wanted that. I would have been less alone, less numb. Perhaps we would have even been stronger together. We might even have been able to change something. I waited for you. I hoped you would come. When they called us up, my first reaction was to look for you. I wanted to make sure that everything was, in fact, real. To be certain that this wasn't all a bad dream. To see this madness unfolding, but on somebody else's face. I wanted a mirror, yes, and you were that mirror. You had to be. I needed someone to be. I needed someone to tell me they actually understood what was happening. More profoundly than human reasoning can even understand. I wanted someone as capable as I am of tolerating reality, and yet unable to turn away from it. It's easy to suffer from something you don't understand. You just let yourself get swept away by it. But to suffer because you understand, to get answers, to look at the world and see it for what it is, that's real suffering. I hoped you would come because nobody else could have felt that pain. Real pain. The kind that you just can't escape. The kind that won't be hidden or tamed or alleviated. Not the pain that you simply endure, but real pain, the pain that grows with every second because you refuse to give in. If only you knew how much I hoped you would come.

Why didn't you come? What were you hoping for, what were you thinking? That the simple act of not looking would *alleviate the pain? What were you thinking? That not looking would somehow save you? What is there left to save for you, for either of us at this point? Perhaps you suffered even more than I did. I hope so. There is always a debt to be paid in the avoidance of suffering.*

Truth be told, I'm not sure what motivates me to write to you . . . I've been speaking to you about us and our pain, about us as we face pain, but I am not as naive as those who believe that pain can be conquered by sharing it. I'm not looking to conquer it. I'm looking to survive, and pain always wins. To survive pain is not to conquer it—only to push it forward on the path of life. Push it further ahead. But still, we walk toward it. How sad we are. And then, one day, we find ourselves unable to catch up to it. We are dead. We can never triumph against heartache; only be outlived by it, despite ourselves.

You should have come. Your son was waiting for you too. I saw it in his eyes. He didn't see his father, he was looking for his mother. I noticed the loneliness and sadness in his gaze. I looked at him. He was beautiful. He wanted to see you. I'm not his mother, and even though I looked at him the same way I looked at my own daughter Aïda, with all the love I could summon, there was nothing I could do. My love could never make up for your absence. They were beautiful together . . .

I cried and dragged myself through the mud. I went back into the crowd hoping, up until the last moment, that something would save them. That you would come, that God, God . . . But nothing happened. Nobody came. God . . .

I watched until the very end. And until the very end, they held each other's hands.

CHAPTER 6

The sight that welcomed Malamine and Vieux Faye as they entered the tavern didn't startle them in the slightest. This was what they were expecting to find. Their faces didn't show any signs of surprise. After greeting the crowd who appeared to have frozen upon their arrival, both men walked naturally toward the back of the room. Those they greeted politely responded, *"Aleïkum Salam."* Then, the cheery ambiance of *Jambaar*[17]—this was the tavern's name— returned, filled with bursts of laughter and joyous roars.

Jambaar was, without a doubt, the only place in Kalep that was still occasionally busy at night. It was located on the first floor of a house in the heart of the poor neighborhoods in the south of the city. The outside was nothing special, but the interior, though far from rich or luxurious, was kept to a standard of style and cleanliness that would restore dignity to even the most run-down house. In this neighborhood—which contained many of these houses—*Jambaar* felt palatial despite its modest appearance. The tavern seemed to have been there forever. Though it was unclear exactly how, it was one of those popular places that conveyed all the things that gave a city its unique identity: its charms, mysteries, virtues, vices—a place, in short, that was clearly loved. Everyone still remembers the fierce rivalry between the tavern and Ndey Joor Camara's

---

[17] The valiant warrior; the hero.

restaurant. But this so-called rivalry existed only in conversations between the people of Kalep. In reality, what appeared to be a rivalry was in fact an implicit collaboration: the *Çinn-gui* fed Kalep's people during the day; *Jambaar* got them drunk at night. The latter quenched their thirst, the former satisfied their hunger. And that was that. Unfortunately, this vital collaboration lasted but a few weeks; for the reasons we all know, the *Çinn-gui* had closed its doors.

Jambaar had opened forty years earlier, during a time when the city was still a mere village that lacked electricity, paved streets, and even a health clinic. People died young and some said jokingly that this is what the Good Lord wanted. One could say that *Jambaar* had seen Kalep blossom, grow, and expand to become what is today, one of the treasures of Bandiani and Sumal. The tavern was a witness. The man who ran *Jambaar* from the very beginning and who had refused to give it up was an old man, known in city and in the rest of the country as Père Badji.

Though he was one of Kalep's oldest residents, not much was known about him. The man was a misanthrope in the truest sense of the term. This was quite a paradox for someone whose tavern gathered the biggest crowds in the city. How can you be a misanthrope when a sea of humans shows up at your door every night? What a mystery. That's exactly what Père Badji was: a mystery. Nobody really knew him; he, however, knew everyone. He went out little, spoke only when he could not do otherwise, lived alone, walked alone, seemed to be moved by nothing, and yet paid attention to everything. He was seventy years old: his age was known because he had been forced to disclose it to a police officer, who later spread rumors, in order to receive his ID. However, Père Badji looked fifteen years younger, which was a testament to his strict lifestyle. He had a harsh face; his forehead was scattered with a few deep wrinkles, which seemed to hide traces of an astounding life. His hair, whitened from the years, was perhaps the only real indication of his advanced age, because his body was still strong. Nevertheless, he had a slight limp in his left leg. While this handicap might've hindered him physically, it took nothing away from the mysterious aura that enveloped him on each rare occasion that he left his house to walk around Kalep. His limp made him even more intriguing, and one could only imagine what kind of hurdle had weakened a man who seemed to be made of brass. The oldest people in Kalep, those who had witnessed the opening of *Jambaar*, would tell stories about how Père Badji used to be a soldier and had received a bullet in his thigh before being discharged. They'd add that the bullet was still in his thigh. True or false, the story was simply unverifiable: Père Badji had no friends, and those who tried to get close to him—there had been many in the past twenty years—had stumbled over his silence, his terrible gaze, and his barely polite but sharp words indicating that he wanted to be left alone. The curious people of Kalep sought to uncover this man's secret. Some used children to try and coax him, but Père Badji gave them candy and asked them to go and play elsewhere. Others tried to soften him with gifts: he'd pretend he didn't enjoy gifts and politely refuse them. Finally, some went as far as to try and use the ultimate weapon of seduction. He'd gallantly refuse the women who were not his type, welcomed those who were into his bed, all the while withholding any sort of confession. The rare few who did manage to make it into his room—this happened over thirty years ago in the first years that followed his arrival in Kalep—all came back with the same three pieces of information: he lives humbly, always offers something after the night is over, and makes love sweetly and silently. That's pretty much all that was known about him.

As for the rest of it, he was always seen standing behind the counter, calm, smoking his pipe, taking orders and filling cups.

He didn't speak. As lively and loud as his tavern was, he was impenetrable, always busy with his work. When it was time to close up, he'd go upstairs to his apartment.

Jambaar was a large, circular room lit by neon lamps which diffused a vivid white light. It contained a few roughly carved ebony-colored tables which were scattered throughout, as well as chairs made from the same wood. At the back of the room there were two large windows which appeared to be sealed off, as was the door next to them. Just to the right of the entrance, a staircase led to the second floor where Père Badji lived. While they were clean, the floor tiles had nevertheless begun to crack in certain areas. Adjoining the ramp of the staircase and occupying a large part of the room's right wing was a counter that molded to the shape of the room and formed a semicircle. It was a long bar; its dark wood must have been magnificent in the old days, even though the rest of the decor was quite basic. It was lined with tall, matching stools. Behind the counter was a refrigerator containing beverages and a sink where Père Badji would do the dishes between shifts. There was also a cupboard with countless glasses of all types and purposes. Above all this clutter, you could see an old hunting rifle with a carved bore. It was suspended and supported by two iron hooks which were fixed to the wall: one carried the barrel, the other the butt. This weapon contributed to the mystery of the place, and many conversations as to its origin and function—whether practical or simply decorative—had ended inconclusively. Père Badji never intervened. To the left of the tavern's entryway was a small sign which displayed the menu and prices. Beneath it was a red door that carried the following straightforward inscription: *"Toilets. Keep them clean or I'll close them like the ones in the back."*

This was, more or less, the layout of *Jambaar*, whose owner was Père Badji, and where the atmosphere was cheerful.

But this had been before the Brotherhood arrived. Because

once it did, whatever it was that contributed to the beauty of the place was lost, and nobody knew why or how. And yet, the Brotherhood had done nothing, officially or unofficially, that could possibly explain why the tavern was becoming increasingly deserted.

They were just there.

They patrolled the streets silently and menacingly, like scarecrows. They were there with their turbans, their jeeps, and their weapons. That was enough to harden a man's heart, to spook his soul, to tear apart a community. And that's what happened. Some locals continued to go there from time to time, but without any hope of being reacquainted with the cheerful atmosphere of the past. Then the first stonings and executions began. From that moment, people stopped going altogether.

Père Badji had observed all of this with lucidity. He quickly understood the link between his declining business and the Brotherhood. But, as usual, he said nothing. What would have been the point of speaking (again, the futility of language)? Even as he lost his clients, Père Badji didn't close the tavern, but he did let go of the two servers who occasionally helped him. They didn't know much about Père Badji either, other than the fact that he was an honest owner. He'd stay open every night and smoke his pipe. He spent entire evenings like this. Alone. Sometimes a beggar would come inside the tavern and ask for something to eat or drink. Père Badji would give him a coffee to warm him up and offer him whatever was left of his meal. This strange situation lasted a few months.

Then, slowly but surely, the tavern came back to life, but with a very different kind of energy. A new clientele became invested in the tavern. The Brotherhood's faithful servants in Kalep started to come more often. They had heard about the place from the locals who had recommended it if ever they wanted to warm up or drink during their nightly patrol. And the locals would give them directions. At first, it was just the night patrol. But then, as rumor spread, the other members of the Brotherhood based in the city began to meet up at the tavern as often as their duties allowed. Usually they came at night or the morning after big events, for example after winning a battle or taking over a new territory. Or after they'd executed someone. On those nights, they'd come and drink and celebrate, cheery, joyous, carefree, and drunk.

CHAPTER 7

When Malamine and Vieux Faye entered *Jambaar*, the place was filled with the Brotherhood's fighters. They were assembled in small groups and primarily occupied the center of the room, which had the best lighting. Their faces were visible because they had removed their turbans, which usually hid them. They drank, smoked, and chatted.

Glimmers of joy and confidence could be seen on every face in this small military group.

Upon walking by them, Malamine and Vieux Faye overheard a few words of what seemed to be a joyful conversation:

"She had beautiful breasts. I wanted to shoot them since I couldn't touch them! If you had seen them up close, *wallah*, you would've done the same, and . . ."

The two men heard nothing more, as they passed the group without turning back and walked toward a table close to the two windows and the closed bathroom. The group of men burst out laughing right as Malamine and Vieux Faye got comfortable . . .

It was nearly two in the morning when Abdel Karim's men left the tavern with big smiles that betrayed their good mood. They drank a lot. Père Badji waited calmly for the noise of the car to fade toward the East before joining the two men at the back of the room. They hadn't left their table. They had ordered two cups of *ataya*[18] and stayed there, exchanged a few

---

[18] Tea.

words in hushed voices, clearly indifferent to the fighters' laughter and conversations.

When Père Badji reached the table, both men stood.

"I thought they'd never leave," said Vieux Faye. "And on top of it spending all night talking about an execution, a murder! I don't know how you can put up with these assassins as often as you do."

The old man didn't respond and took a few puffs from his pipe, observing Vieux Faye casually. Vieux Faye was a light-skinned man, approximately forty years old with sudden and nervous gestures. He had quit smoking two years earlier, and despite a few relapses during the first few months, he slowly managed to resist temptation. Today he no longer smoked but was always frantically chewing gum. The permanent chewing added movement to his already worried and agitated face, and together all of this made him seem like a hurried man. Or worse: like a worried man.

"In any case, thank you, Père Badji, for having us once again. I don't know what would become of us if it weren't for you."

"You're welcome, Malamine."

The man who had entered with Vieux Faye, and who had just exchanged a few words with Père Badji, bowed his head as a gesture of gratitude toward their host. Malamine was tall, and his deep voice conveyed a sense of serenity, a stark contrast to the agitation of Vieux Faye. He was imposing and reassuring. Even Père Badji didn't seem completely immune to the charisma of this man, one of the rare men with whom he agreed to exchange a few words.

"I assume we are the first to arrive. I hope the others will come. I would hate it if you picked me up and drove me all the way to Soro for nothing," said Vieux Faye.

"Don't worry, Vieux Faye. They will come. They're true friends, you know that. Before arriving in Soro, I passed by

Bantika. I warned everyone. Those who live in Kalep are also aware, of course."

"These are trustworthy people, surely. But above all else, they're human. One must never completely trust men. They are always changing, and for pathetic reasons. So imagine the challenge of this meeting. Just imagine."

"Vieux . . ."

"I'm skeptical."

Knowing his friend's profound skepticism, Malamine didn't answer and smiled. He turned once again to Père Badji, who was looking at them silently, even somewhat indifferently.

"We're going to go down to prepare the room, Père Badji. The others should not be long. Wait until they're all here, close the bar, and join us, please. We're waiting for you."

Père Badji simply nodded, turned around, and slowly went back to the counter.

"What a strange old man!"

"You can doubt anyone, even me, even yourself if it amuses you, but not him. He's the most important one of us."

Vieux Faye shrugged his shoulders incredulously and followed his friend. Malamine headed toward the closed door. Once he was in front of it, he reached for the doorknob, turned it, and gave the door a hard push. The door opened and offered the shadowy view of the unused toilets.

"Père Badji may be trustworthy, but he should think about adding some light to this place."

"That would be useless, this room isn't important."

Malamine waited a few seconds for his eyes to adapt to the darkness. The room was square and the layout extremely simple. Against the wall on the right-hand side was a row of narrow booths with toilets. They were separated by thin wooden dividers where people had drawn and written obscenities, love notes, phone numbers, insults, or just initials. On the left and parallel to the booths were four urinals mounted to the wall;

and on the wall in the back, the one facing the entry door, one could see two sinks with a cracked mirror hanging above them. Malamine headed toward the booth at the end of the row and opened it. It was empty: the toilet had been moved. There was a wooden hatch on the floor where the base of the toilet should have been. Malamine grabbed the hatch, effortlessly lifted what seemed to be a heavy flap, and propped it against the wall.

At both men's feet there was an opening to a dark cavity. Malamine fumbled for a moment on the partition wall until he found a button. He pressed it. A white light sprang from the darkness and revealed the steps of an underground staircase.

Without a word, as if they were used to this sort of maneuver, the two men went down into the basement.

CHAPTER 8

Everyone had come. They were there, in this little underground room, the basement of *Jambaar* which they had managed, through patience, work, diligence, and discretion, to convert into their headquarters. It had taken them almost a year to complete, but they'd done it. Though small, the room had a certain charm and was unassailable. This was perhaps the safest place in Kalep, even though the people in the room had taken great risks to be there.

Malamine had the idea for this setup after he witnessed an execution for the first time.

The woman they executed was accused of prostitution. She was buried up to the waist, then Captain Abdel Karim came to read some sort of death warrant. A pile of stones had already been prepared. Malamine saw the whole crowd. He saw the woman, who was crying, begging, weeping. He noticed the members of the crowd, all drunk, picking up stones and throwing them at the woman. He heard the condemned woman's final cry, a cry from which all humanity had been removed. Malamine watched her die. It had only lasted a few seconds (who could ever pinpoint the exact moment a life departs from the soul and body?): after this cry, she lifted her eyes to the sky and whispered something. Then a single stone, whose aim was more precise than the others, hit her forehead. The woman fell forward and stopped moving.

CHAPTER 9

This alleged whore's execution not only bothered Malamine: it also scared him, and it's this fear which later prompted him to act. He wasn't afraid of being in that woman's place one day, or of seeing a loved one in her place (his death or that of his loved ones through stoning was far from being a certainty), but because in that moment right before her death, the woman had lifted her eyes to the sky and whispered something inaudible, something nobody else had heard. This was the cause of Malamine's unquestionable, immediate, and profound fear. The woman's last words, uttered on the brink of death, frightened Malamine. Their scope was breathtaking and their meaning mysterious: was it a prayer, a regret, a curse, a calling, a memory? Malamine couldn't bear the thought that nobody had heard these words, the very last of somebody's life. The fact that this woman had been forced to talk to herself, to confide in herself, and to rely on her own loneliness terrified him. Once more, the woman's final words had been pointless—in the sense that no other human being had heard or answered them. This futility (this forced silence) is what scared Malamine, and what later made him want to resist.

Those who submit to tyranny and those who stand up against it are united by fear, cold-blooded fear. There are no heroes or cowards, and as a result courage has no more meaning or value than cowardice. At first, there are only those who are scared and who decide to do something with their fear:

they fly with the wings that fear has granted them, or they stay on the ground, paralyzed, their feet in shackles.

Malamine feared the futility of language in the same way that others around him feared being beaten or bullied. His fear was legitimate; perhaps even inevitable in his situation.

He had experienced the good fear: the one which, in one way or another, was related to language, and to the possibility of its loss.

CHAPTER 10

A t first, Malamine didn't know what to do. He had almost given up out of desperation a few times. He was ready to surrender and recant his oath, ready to resign. But every time his indignation lessened, another public execution would occur, and he would attend, even though he was repulsed by it. With every stone tossed, every shot fired, every cry from the crowd, every grin from the executioners, every tortured victim's groan, and with every death, he gained new strength. While the others cried, tossed stones, Malamine would fall to his knees amid their frantic gesticulations. He would stand up only after the crowd, breathless, panting, foam on their lips, ceased their cries. Then he'd scrutinize every face in the dispersing crowd, none of which showed any signs of happiness or disgust, but simply a sense of incomprehension, of indifference, and of unsustainable irresponsibility.

He wanted to act. He needed help. This is how he found it.

Malamine liked to walk at night. Under the gleaming stars, he found the calm and silence he needed to strengthen his hopes and calm his fears. Human consciousness neither rises nor falls entirely on its own; to exalt in its loneliness is to offer God a window into the soul, to melt into a moment when the world's intelligence is as perfect and just as can be: at night. It was during one of these grandiose nights that Malamine had once again found help. He was wandering aimlessly in the streets of Kalep and made it to the City Hall square without realizing it. There, he noticed a shadow moving slowly. With the confidence known only to insomniacs and lonely wanderers, he decided to walk up to the shadow. He had to go toward this man and nowhere else. He caught up with him in no time: the man was limping slightly and did not turn around, even though Malamine made no efforts to muffle his steps. Once Malamine was a few feet away, the man finally stopped.

"Who are you?" he said.

"My name is Malamine."

"That does not tell me who you are."

"I'm a doctor. Here, actually, in the hospital of Kalep."

"What do you want from me?"

"I'm not sure. I saw you and I walked toward you. I'm alone, and so are you."

"I've always been alone. I don't like to talk to other men, sir. Talk to God. He is there, in his entirety, everywhere in the night. He is patient. I am not."

"I need your help."

"I help no one."

Malamine was silent and looked around. Next to them, a mound of stones stood out in the darkness.

"They've already prepared the stones for tomorrow."

The man in front of him did not answer and kept his back turned.

"I need help to fight back. I'm alone. And nobody can fight these men alone. I want to fight back against the Brotherhood. They're going to kill someone else tomorrow. I don't want to keep watching without doing anything about it. I can't take it anymore."

The man turned around slowly. Because of the darkness, Malamine could not make out his face.

"How do you know I'm not one of those people you want to fight back against?"

"I don't. But I wanted to talk to someone, and I saw you."

"You're careless, my son."

Malamine was quiet.

"What do you need?" asked the old man after a few minutes.

"A safe place, and a friend."

"I don't have any friendship to offer you."

"The place will do."

"Come tomorrow at this time to *Jambaar*. I am the owner."

"You are the famous Père Badji?"

The man didn't answer. He had turned around and was beginning to walk away. His limp gave his gait a worrying pace. Malamine understood that the conversation was over. He was ready to turn back when a sudden urge overtook him.

"What did they take from you?"

Père Badji stopped abruptly, as if Malamine's question had triggered a violent shock. A cold wind from the desert up north blew through the square. A few seconds passed. Père Badji responded.

"My dog. They burned him."

Then the old man continued to walk. Before heading home, Malamine watched him disappear into the night. That's how he met Père Badji.

The next day, they met again. Père Badji mentioned the basement of *Jambaar*, for which he no longer had much use. Originally, it was meant to serve as a warehouse for the beverage crates. But Père Badji finally changed his mind and decided to close it and build restrooms on top. The night they saw each other again, Père Badji armed himself with an ice axe, huge hammers, wheelbarrows, and other tools: to get to the abandoned room they would have to dig, but additional hands would be needed to clean, rebuild, rearrange, and furnish. It would be slow, long, difficult.

Malamine called his friends, those he thought would be willing to help. They had all accepted. Over the course of a few months, they met once a week at *Jambaar* in the dead of night.

Not all lived in Kalep, but they came regardless. This strange procession lasted a long time. The room was built slowly, despite the risks involved, the Brotherhood's patrols, and the fear of being caught. Some days, they couldn't work because the patrols stayed at the tavern until late or were roaming the neighborhood too frequently. But they managed. One year after the construction began, the room was ready. They had furnished it sparsely. They met there a few times to discuss their approach and strategy. Now the time had come to act.

That was the subject of tonight's meeting. Sitting in the middle of his group of friends, Malamine was thinking. He was thinking about the woman they had executed and what she could have said before her death.

CHAPTER 11

T hey were all there. All six of them who had come to his rescue, all six of them who had built this room with their bare hands, patiently and with unwavering sacrifice, and more importantly, who had accepted to fight alongside Malamine.

There was Déthié. Déthié the warrior thinker, the ideologist—Déthié, the passionate one. Déthié his friend from his youth. From the day they met at the University of Bantika, Malamine had always admired him. Even back then, he had this fire, this volcanic accent in his voice. It was hypnotizing. He was a man of rare eloquence and refused to admit that words and speeches were but the product of a stylistic and rhetorical impulse. He was always making sure that the beauty of his words, the splendor of their mysterious and powerful rhythm, was in perfect harmony with the truth of his ideas. Déthié was captivating. He was, however, a man with an understated if not unattractive physique; small, short legs, square at the base, rather robust, bald. His face was adorned with an extraordinary mustache. But as soon as he spoke, he became a giant. People listened to him without ever interrupting. At the university, he was always at the forefront: leader of strikes, responsible for student committees, spokesman for different protests. But he was not the kind of leader who only dealt with the formal and administrative side of his tasks. Above all, Déthié was a fighter, and he fought for his ideas. In fact, oftentimes he liked to finish his speeches with these words: "To die for one's ideas is the most honorable death, because it means that one had ideas in the first place. This is a great privilege in a world filled with cowardice, a world in which people no longer think or think backwards." He was a man whose age had not softened him in the slightest: on the contrary, the violence with which he defended his ideas and the enthusiasm of his character had only increased with age. He was now a professor at the University of Bantika. What an odd and ironic twist of fate for a man who despised conformity and restraint. "I am at the University in order to rehabilitate a tradition of freedom and subversion, nothing more," he'd repeat to his students and to anybody else who wanted to know. Déthié accepted Malamine's request without any hesitation. He was the first one, actually. Malamine was happy he was there. This small group needed a thinker. Déthié, this extraordinary and flamboyant man, as big as a god, revolutionary in his soul and passionate in his ideals, was this thinker.

Malamine was the group's soul.

Codou was its heart. Codou. Déthié's wife. If Déthié was still alive, it was thanks to this angel in a woman's body. Déthié's temperament, when let loose, was quick to openly oppose the Brotherhood. He needed someone to rein him in, a bridle, a blinder, an enclosure. Codou was all of these things. The first time one saw Codou, one couldn't help but wonder by what spell she had come to marry Déthié. It seemed that she was everything he wasn't. Shy, mute even: the rare times she spoke publicly gave away a voice whose softness was just as striking as Déthié's was violent. Not only that, her voice revealed the calm and stable nature of her character, the clarity and depth of her mind, and the precision and power of her ideas. She spoke little but well. She was always thinking, and thinking justly. Malamine still remembers how a few years back, Déthié had succumbed to Codou's charm. Though she rarely spoke at the time, she attended all of the meetings of the various committees Déthié led. She had a certain demeanor which only those few who are always thinking—and thinking deeply—can convey. Malamine believed that Codou and himself were very much alike in that respect. As for the rest, Codou was Déthié without the ardor of his outbursts. Her behavior was cool, calm, and collected, which perhaps made it even more extraordinary and intriguing than her husband's. Their love was passionate and rare. Their temperaments complemented one another, and they shared identical ideas. This kind of love, while neither exclusive nor jealous, is nevertheless often all-encompassing. In fact, Codou and Déthié admitted they had room neither in their relationship nor in their hearts to have children together. They never conceived. Because of her past life as a bookseller, Codou had a rich cultural background which allowed her to assist her husband in university-related affairs. Ever since the Brotherhood had arrived, she closed down the bookshop because she refused to uphold such a noble profession in a country where terror reigns and blood is being shed. She spent her days amongst books, reading, taking notes, and meditating. She was a modern philosopher. She agreed to fight back without any hesitation. She was the intelligent heart of the group, and one of its two women.

The second was Madjigueen Ngoné. Another name for beauty. She worked as an IT specialist at the hospital of Kalep. This is where she met Malamine. Like every other person who met her, Malamine was first and foremost struck by the incredible beauty of this woman who was not even thirty years old. Her body was a divine gift to the human eye. Her skin begged to be touched. But Madjigueen Ngoné's most striking feature was her eyes . . . She had big, bright eyes in which furious storms erupted. Anybody who saw those eyes and the gaze they struck immediately grasped Madjigueen Ngoné's untamable character. She was a wild soul with a deceptively soft and gentle presence. Young, beautiful, seemingly naïve, she came off easy, dumb, disingenuous and superficial. How many men had tried to sleep with her only to be turned down in an equally abrupt and humiliating manner? Just as Madjigueen Ngoné's independence had taught her to make fun of men, it had also taught her to be wary of them. She used her charm not only to better ridicule them, but also to make it clear that she refused to be objectified. Malamine was most likely the only person in Kalep's hospital, along with Alioune, whom she respected and was friendly with. In the context of their work at the hospital, Malamine interacted with her appropriately, made her feel like more than just a pretty face, didn't make her aware of her beauty, and never treated her more favorably than he treated others, something she had learned to recognize as subtle flirting. Because she wished for nothing more than to be treated like everyone else, Madjigueen Ngnoné appreciated this. And thus their friendship was born. No one knew if she had a family, not even Malamine. She wasn't from around there. People just knew she lived alone. Her wild nature, her love of independence, was not enough to convince Malamine to ask for Madjigueen Ngnoné's help. But one night as he was strolling around Kalep, he spotted her. She was carrying food and clothing and was going to see Kalep's beggars. She'd offer one of them a garment, another some rice cakes. Malamine followed her at a distance, because he felt like she was trying to hide. She'd turn her head when people walked by, as if she feared that others might see her, such a tough, unique, and proud woman stooping down to help Kalep's poorest. Some might have seen this as vanity, but Malamine saw it as kindness. Well, in his mind, any generosity of heart was a blow to the Brotherhood. The following day, Malamine asked for her help. She accepted.

Finally, there was Alioune. He was the youngest of the group. But was he not, paradoxically, also the oldest at heart? Alioune hoped for nothing, believed in nothing. Though he had only witnessed nineteen winters, he expected nothing from this existence. He also worked at Kalep's hospital, as a nurse. An impenetrable and permanent sadness veiled his face. The only time he didn't seem engulfed by an all-consuming sadness was when he was reading. Malamine noticed that this melancholic young man never laughed; one day, intrigued, he spoke to him:

"I've never seen you smile, Alioune."

"It's because I never smile, doctor."

"But why . . . ?" began Malamine.

Alioune interrupted him.

"Don't ask me why. Don't tell me that at my age I should smile. Don't tell me that young people are happy and bright and that I'm not allowed to be sad. Age has nothing to do with it. What I see is neither happy nor bright and gives me no reason to smile."

"You seem hopeless."

"I don't even have that luxury, doctor. I get by any way I can, in an enclosed, dry, abandoned land. I'm not hopeless, I don't know what that means. Hopelessness implies that one was once hopeful. I don't remember a time when I was still hopeful. Did that time ever exist?"

"You're too young to be unhappy."

"I'm not unhappy."

"What's the difference between no longer believing in anything and being unhappy?"

"I believe in something, doctor. I believe in poetry. And it's not a sham. I'm not a hopeless romantic. I don't play. I don't pretend. I grew up quickly, faster than anybody, and I've seen just as many atrocities. I have the right—yes, the right—to no longer believe in intelligence and human dignity, and to believe only in poetry."

"Despite your efforts, you can't keep yourself from believing in mankind. You're a nurse."

"So?"

"That says a lot."

The conversation ended there. But from that day on, the two men grew closer. Over time, Malamine got to know his young friend. When, one day, Malamine asked him to help fight back against the Brotherhood, Alioune simply replied: "I have nothing to lose, and I can gain the privilege of finally getting out of here. You can count on me." That was Alioune: a young boy, too old for his own good, made brave from sorrow, appalled by the customary barbarism, with no faith in anything but the rare beauties in life. Like fireflies, these beauties soared in the midst of ruins, shone just long enough to be admired by those who still knew how to look for them, and then vanished.

A journal. They needed a journal to bear witness to the barbarism. A journal to reflect on the madness of terrorism. An underground journal. That's the decision they had come to after many previous meetings. To create a journal, distribute it all over the province. They would risk being caught but they'd do it regardless. And to contemplate the situation from every angle: political, religious, philosophical, military, ideological, and simply human. To contemplate each angle in its entirety: from its origin to its potential consequences, without forgetting the facts in all of their complexity. Ultimately, a journal in which to say no. They had all agreed on this principle. Today would be the first session of work.

All seven friends were there. Déthié, who wrote half of the articles. Codou, who corrected them and enriched them with references if necessary. Madjigueen Ngnoné, who took the finished texts and created the proper layout. Vieux Faye was in charge of printing and binding them. Alioune was responsible for illustrating the texts with drawings or photos—if he managed to take any without getting caught. Père Badji had to take care of the logistics. Malamine wrote the other articles.

He looked at them and, in that moment, his six friends

suddenly appeared giant and dazzling to him. It was as if each friend embodied one of the great aspects of Man. His eyes grew teary.

Déthié was Freedom. Codou was Justice. Madjigueen Ngoné was Equality. Vieux was Denial. Alioune was Beauty. Père Badji was Mystery. Man was all of these qualities together.

What about him? Who was he?

"Stop staring at us with that empty gaze, young man. It's time to get to work, don't you think?"

Malamine smiled. Déthié was right. He gestured to his friends to take a seat.

The work began. They were unsure how many nights it would take, but they got to it. They made the decision to fight back and transform their fear. That's the most important and, surely, the most difficult thing to do for a man in shackles who dreams of his freedom.

CHAPTER 12

M y name is Sadobo. But you already knew this. It felt good to read your letter. Answering you will allow me to convince myself that I'm not dead yet.

I don't know how you were able to go. I don't know. And I can't know. I resent you, too. It's my turn to ask you the same question: What were you hoping you would gain by going? Were you trying to be brave? Did you think you could outsmart suffering? Did you really believe that by facing your suffering head-on, you'd become accustomed to it? Did you really think that your presence could save them? Save you? You're so naïve.

You talk about being strong. Why? Why try to be strong when you know deep inside that everything is falling apart? It's impossible to remain strong when both of our children are dead. All we can do is try. But in this case, to try is to gamble with that which you'll never achieve. These days we have too much faith in Man, far too much. We overestimate him, place him on the same pedestal as God, or at the very least grant him the same degree of power. The will to defy the world, destiny, events, God, it ends up becoming most inhuman. We're instructed to remain strong above all else. But why is weakness forbidden? Why believe that a human being can overcome anything? We need to accept defeat. Accept it without thinking of ourselves as heroes, without trying to justify it. We need to lose. To know how to let go, fall, collapse, and break entirely. We're ashamed of our suffering. Our pain is *quick, superficial. It lacks depth. And that's our true suffering. We want to be heroes but we don't have the means. We want to be tragic without the greatness of a tragedy.*

I know that everything within me is destroyed, annihilated. So I'd rather let go. You believe that suffering cannot be overcome. I believe that it can, but under the sole condition that it kills us first. Coming back to life, that's what it requires.

That's why I didn't go. I'm not trying to convince you. I think we're both right, and that we're both wrong. You went to face the pain and exposed yourself to its terrible bite. I waited for it and let its venom rise. We're not all that different, I think . . .

Our children are dead, Aïssata. Your daughter is dead, and my son is dead. There's no point in telling me how it happened: I felt the horror of it in the deepest parts of my flesh. We must live with this death. Not accept it, because accepting it is impossible. But live with it, in spite of it. Nothing tells us that we will be able to overcome this. Pain is unpredictable. We think we're healing, and then one blow is enough to reopen the wound.

I miss Lamine, Aïssata. I miss him so much that it makes my stomach hurt. I feel like I'm carrying him inside me a second time.

Write to me again.

Sadobo

A t the market, Idrissa Camara struggled to make his way through the crowd. Once he arrived at City Hall, he had no choice but to get off his bike and walk alongside it. He was trying his best to move forward despite all the obstacles standing in his way in the midst of distracting sounds and overwhelming but enticing smells. He blamed himself for ending up in this human prison. The suffocating afternoon heat added to his misery. He had forgotten it was Thursday, and that Thursday is market day in Kalep. It was also the most popular market in the whole province. It was an opportunity for Bandiani's merchants to grow their businesses by selling their wares. The farmers sold their crops, breeders their livestock, and fishermen the fruit of their expeditions far into the Atlantic. And everyone came together with no divisions. Tables of fruits and vegetables stood next to tables of fish and meat. Piles of candy and different grains were laying next to each other on the ground amid whirls of dust. And around all of this, like a pen made of animals surrounding a flock of humans, herds of cows, goats, sheep, and camels got friendly with each other. Despite its size, the entire square was filled.

Once in a while, Idrissa would ring the bell on his bike. He realized this gesture was pretty useless and foolish, even absurd and ridiculous among the cries, conversations, bargaining, scandals, thefts, deafening roars, shouts, bleats, and enormous ruminations. On Thursdays, Kalep became a giant souk—a vortex that ingested all of the activities that were occurring in proximity to its gaping mouth.

Idrissa was unsure how to feel about the surreal atmosphere of the market; it gave him the impression that Kalep's people enjoyed the circumstances they were living in. A few of them had taken part in the executions, but how could he find out why? And, more importantly, how could he find out if they had any regrets? He had no way of knowing. Their faces revealed nothing, offered nothing which might be available for interpretation. Each had his or her reasons, fears, and doubts which nobody else knew. That's what frightened him. The thick mystery of mankind never dissipated. Idrissa surrendered.

He glanced at his watch and gasped: he should have been home a long time ago. His mother was probably worried.

* * *

Ndey Joor Camara was standing at her doorstep, anxiously looking out at the street.

"Where is he? Where did he go? Nobody needs two hours to run an errand. I hope nothing happened to him. But where is he? The food has been ready for half an hour; it's going to get cold and I'll have to reheat it. It's a shame because a dish always loses some of its flavor when you reheat it before it has even been served. A reheated dish is only good the next day. Oh well, I'll reheat it. But where is he?" she wondered.

She didn't hear the sound of the car arriving on the side of the road. A loud honk startled her and made her jump. She turned around. Two men with turbans exited the back of a gray jeep. One of them was armed. Ndey Joor Camara's face hardened. She remained still and watched the three men come toward her.

"*Assalamu Aleïkum*, Adjaratou," said the shorter of the two soldiers. He was stocky, like a spring, ready to straighten at any moment. His voice was hoarse, brutal, unpleasant.

Ndey Joor Camara did not answer. The man continued.

"Why aren't you covered, Adjaratou?"

Mechanically, with the innocence of a naughty child caught breaking the rules, Ndey Joor Camara touched her head with a graceful gesture. She did so almost to convince herself that her head was, in fact, bare. In all of her anxiety, she had forgotten to put on her veil, which she usually never parted from, not even at home. Her hair was very dark and reached her shoulders. It had been years since she last cut or braided it. Instead, she would comb it briefly and cover it with a veil that she removed only before going to sleep. Her hand fell and she looked at the man who spoke to her, without saying a word. She didn't seem frightened, and there was even a sense of serenity in her gaze.

"But where is he? Where is Idrissa?"

The soldier was trying to intimidate her, but she was thinking about her son because she loved him.

"Why don't you answer me, woman? I asked you a question, didn't I? You want me to beat you, bitch? Are you tongue-tied?"

He came forward and looked even more like a venomous cane toad crouching, ready to pounce. The other man, who was wearing his weapon across his body, hadn't moved. He was watching the scene unfold with disinterest.

"Where is your veil, you old whore? Aren't you ashamed at your age to be out like this, bareheaded? What kind of example are you setting for your younger sisters? You and all those like you shame our religion and our Lord. *Çaga!*"[19]

He spit on the ground forcefully.

Ndey Joor Camara remained silent and did not move her eyes away from the man who was threatening and reprimanding her.

[19] Whore.

"Answer, tramp! Where is your veil?"

By that point, he was yelling. His eyes were bloodshot and two veins appeared on his temples. The children who were playing in the street had now gathered around them. They were watching the scene with a sense of curiosity, though it was unclear if it was fearful or playful. Soon, a few neighboring adults, alerted by the strange and isolated shouts, joined the swarm of children. The street, no longer animated by the children's squawking, was overtaken by a sudden silence. Men and women encircled Ndey Joor Camara and the two soldiers. They were silent, as if torn between fear and curiosity. These incidents had become common occurrences in Kalep; they always provoked feelings of horror mixed with anticipation and prevented their witnesses from moving, even from speaking. Ndey Joor and the two men found themselves in the center of a boxing ring.

People were watching and waiting.

"You're provoking me, you slut! I'll show you what happens when you make fun of me!"

He raised his hand to his right hip where a coiled whip was dangling. The crowd shivered and moved indistinctly: proof of its hesitation. The armed man took his rifle between his hands and held it in a dissuasive stance. At that moment, a third man got out of the vehicle and joined the small group in the center of the ring. He was also armed. He was the driver of the jeep who had, up until that point, remained inside the car.

Ndey Joor Camara was still silent. A mild shiver rushed through her body. But she was silent and looked ahead.

"Old whore! You're going to pay for that!" threatened the armed man.

The leather snake unwound its rings of death, slithered to the ground, and then rose to the sky and spun. It ripped through the air. It made a horrible sound which carried all the rage of the arm that wielded it. Ndey Joor Camara closed her eyes and waited.

"*Yaay booy!*"[20]

She opened her eyes immediately. Rokhaya was running toward her in tears.

"Rokhaya, no, stay inside!" yelled Ndey Joor.

The child disobeyed and threw herself on her mother. Ndey Joor Camara sheltered the child in her arms. This lasted a few seconds.

Then the whip came crashing down.

Once.

She felt her clothes ripping apart, her flesh tearing apart, her blood gushing. She had fallen to her knees without a sound, Rokyaha pressed against her breast. Before the whip hit her, she was able to turn around and offer her back instead. Protecting Rokhaya. Covering her.

Twice.

She felt like her skin was being ripped off. Like her back was bursting into flames. She clenched her teeth and bit her lower lip so hard she nearly tore it off. The bitter taste of her own blood filled her mouth. She could no longer hear anything. Not the insults of the executioner, not the savage cries of the animal lacerating her flesh. All she heard were Rokyaha's cries. She held her even more tightly. And she prayed.

Three times.

The pain stunned her. Her mouth was filled with blood. She moaned but did not yell. Stay silent. Don't say a word. Be quiet. She felt tears escaping her eyes. Rokhaya was screaming.

The fourth time, her strength failed her and she fell forward, Rokhaya under her stomach. Crush her if necessary, but protect her. She could no longer feel anything and was about

[20] Expression that can be translated as "Mother dearest."

to faint. At that moment, as if she'd had a jolt of clarity before falling into unconsciousness, she heard men yelling words that she couldn't make out. She sensed the furious pounding of rapidly approaching steps and the sound of shots being fired. She felt hands—many hands—lifting her and carrying her away.

"Rokhaya . . . My daughter, find my daughter, protect my daughter," she moaned.

"Mom, it's me. Hold on, please."

Ndey Joor Camara, head on fire, half naked, bust bleeding, recognized Idrissa's voice, then fainted.

CHAPTER 14

They buried her.

She was given a tomb together with the right to be buried in the Muslim cemetery. They said it's because I begged, and that my pleading moved them. It's true, I acted like a beggar. Like a dog. Usually, they throw the bodies of those accused of adultery into a ditch that they dug up in the desert. I didn't want Aïda to end up there, surrounded by other rotting bodies at the mercy of scavengers. But they demanded that it be done during the night, protected from prying eyes. They also asked that there be no ceremony. We weren't counting on it anyways. What for? Who would have come? They were all there to see her die. Why would they come to her funeral? I will pray alone for her and for your son.

My husband and I buried her ourselves in the middle of the night. Just the two of us. He rented a cart. We loaded the body onto it. It was starting to decompose. Then we crossed the city and went to the cemetery. My husband had already gone once at dawn with his shovel. He's the one who dug the grave. I asked him to dig a deep one because Aïda's body was really beginning to rot. He dug a deep grave. It was in a corner of the cemetery where there weren't many others. We put her there. We couldn't afford a casket, we're not wealthy enough. We weren't even able to build one for her. It would have taken time and by then the body would have rotted entirely. A few years ago, I bought a long white percale sheet.

It was supposed to be her wedding gift. We used it as her shroud.

It was very difficult to lower her into the grave. The hole was narrow, just wide enough for her body. We didn't think to bring ropes. We stayed there for a long time, trying to think of a solution. My husband did most of the thinking. I stayed in the cart next to her body. He searched for a long time. In vain. We could have widened the hole, so that he could go down into the grave with his daughter's body, but we didn't bring a shovel. He hadn't prepared for that.

We had to let her fall to the bottom of the hole. I froze when I heard the sound it made. I can still hear it. But I didn't shout. I didn't weep. None of it mattered anymore.

We said a prayer for the dead before closing the hole. Because we didn't have a shovel, we had to do it with our hands. It took us time because the hole was deep. Kneeling by the pit, I grabbed some sand and threw it onto the body. I don't know how much time went by before it disappeared entirely, but there came a point when I could no longer see the white percale sheet.

He was in a hurry. He was shaking, tossing one handful of sand after another. He grasped it firmly with both hands, as if eager to hide his daughter's body, this dead flesh, the flesh of his own flesh. He was ashamed of this body. This body that had dishonored him. Hadn't he told his daughter before her execution that he was ashamed of her and that she deserved everything that happened to her?

I looked at him. His forehead was lowered, and he was focusing on the task at hand. He seemed unaware of my presence. Fill. Cover.

A man so handsome, so elegant, so proud, had aged a few years in a matter of days. Now, he was but a shadow of himself.

I watched him for a long time as he filled the pit where he believed he was also burying his grief and shame. I pitied him. Perhaps he was crying silently? I couldn't tell, I couldn't hear anything, and it was dark. The day they killed her, he wept. When they asked the parents to leave the crowd, he refused. I am the one who dragged him out of there. I wanted to try and save my daughter one last time. He had given up on her ever since the execution had been decided. From that day on, he's been gloomy—a prisoner of his own grief. He doesn't look at me anymore. He said that I'm partially responsible for what happened to Aïda. He said I didn't raise her properly.

Is he right, Sadobo? I'm the mother, you know? The mother. That says a great deal. All mothers are guilty. All mothers are guilty.

He cried after the shots were fired. Ever since she died, we barely speak.

I grabbed the sand slowly. Each handful was a goodbye. I was burying myself, too. My husband placed a simple wooden sign on top of the grave. It will be swept far away by the next sandstorm. "To Gassama. 1993–2012." Nothing else.

Something strange happened in my neighborhood yesterday. My neighbor, the only one who came to comfort me before the execution, and the only one to offer condolences, was whipped by the military patrol. They beat her until she fainted. But the craziest part of this story is what happened while they were beating her. People were there, watching the scene unfold. Like at the execution. I'm not sure what got into them exactly, but they were yelling and becoming restless. The executioners threatened them with their weapons, but that didn't stop them from yelling. Then, suddenly and in unison, the people in the crowd threw themselves onto the woman. The militia fired. First in the air. It didn't stop anybody. Then, they pointed their weapons to the crowd, which had come to this woman's rescue, and fired at random. It was surreal. The crowd disarmed the man who was doing the whipping and they began to beat him. A thousand hands hit him, grabbed him, shook him, scratched him; the hands of men, women, and children combined. The same fate awaited the other two men.

Ndey Joor Camara—that's the name of the woman—is now hospitalized. She lost a lot of blood.

Why am I telling you this story?

Because I don't understand. I don't understand why yesterday, the same people who attended the execution of our children decided to save a woman who was being beaten to death. Why did they prevent the beating of a woman but not lift a finger when our children were being executed? I don't understand. I don't understand. I don't want to understand. There is nothing to understand. How can these people, responsible for killing, suddenly rise to rebel against death?

I await your reply, Sadobo.

Aïssata

CHAPTER 15

Alioune was wandering around in his fitted nurse's uniform; its whiteness seemed to mock the filthiness of the place.

Every day, this hospital seemed more dreadful to him. It looked more like a waiting room to the afterlife than a place where people's lives are supposed to be saved. He was pacing through the main corridor, its floor filled with patients. Stretchers were scattered around with men who were sleeping, groaning, crying, hallucinating. These men were wounded, leprous, or amputated, their stumps bloody. Near them, pregnant women, children, and the elderly were lying on the ground, awaiting what vaguely resembled death. The hospital was an enormous living dump . . .

In the midst of it all, when they built up enough courage, a few young interns would roam the area. They could be recognized by their short-sleeved green scrubs and the fear on their inexperienced faces. They seemed to be on the verge of fainting. The area was lit by a dim glow, diffused by a glass roof. If that light did come from a sun, then surely that sun must have also been sick, as its rays lost all of their splendor inside the hospital.

The freshly painted white walls retained a nauseating smell. The vapor of ether, the powerful and intoxicating smell of alcohol, the fragrance of mercurochrome, the stench of wounds, and the fumes of poorly preserved corpses from the morgue all contributed to making Kalep's hospital eerily unusual. It was, in short, a hospital like other hospitals, like those you might find anywhere in the country, and especially in the North: a hospital where one often just comes to die with some illusion of dignity. It was a poor hospital, undermined by the lack of qualified personnel and proper equipment, noteworthy for the decaying state of its materials, marred by the deterioration of its wards, and scarred by the moral penury of those within its vicinity, doctors and patients alike.

Alioune was trying to find some room to pass through a sea of injured people, decimated families, and sick, disoriented patients. Most of them were mutilated: one person was missing a leg, another a forearm; the more unfortunate were missing both legs. In the last few months, the hospital had taken in an increasing number of patients. While the Brotherhood was not undertaking summary executions, it was still conducting what it considered to be appropriate and cautionary mutilations. Clearly, this deterred nobody, since more and more patients continued to arrive. The hospital was welcoming more patients than it had the capacity to treat; it didn't have the means to face such a wave of severely disabled people. There was no more space in the wards or in the hospitalization rooms, so they began to use maintenance closets. But these too filled up very quickly; soon, there was no room left at all. By this point, patients began to crowd the corridors and, finally, the courtyard. Doctors provided care and changed bandages in the open air, without any privacy or semblance of basic hygiene and comfort. The operating rooms were reserved only for the most urgent cases: for those on the brink of death. They had priority. Once you begin to establish a hierarchy among human lives, once you begin to rank people's suffering, to sort through them and find the one who is most deserving of care, once you reach that point, the most difficult part is not determining whether or not your gesture is despicable. In these circumstances, that kind of question is absurd. The hard part is determining, without having to cheat or make concessions, one's degree of responsibility for what led to this situation in the first place. When people's loved ones are suffering, few wonder how they contributed to prevent or encourage that suffering. Alioune hated his colleagues for blaming their situation on History, without wondering for a second what they, individually or collectively, had done to contribute to this outcome. How had this started? What had they done when the Brotherhood was approaching? That's what Alioune was asking himself.

He observed all these disabled people begging at his feet. He wondered if they, too, had applauded a mutilation, a simple act which was now impossible for some of them to do. He wondered if they'd also held stones in their hands and thrown them at a woman who sinned or an unmarried couple. Today they were here, hurting, gruesome, hunchbacked like Quasimodo, transformed forever by the very same people they had once supported.

Once in a while, he'd make eye contact with someone, and that gaze would latch onto him. The gaze implored him, begged for him to help in any way that he could. They were all there lying in the hallway, waiting for somebody to come and tend to them. They had been there for hours, days, sometimes even weeks. Occasionally, a doctor would come and kneel next to one of them. He'd be carrying a small satchel containing a basic first aid kit, enough to cover a wound but barely enough to clean it. Sometimes, a single person or a few people would be called. The chosen few would then stand, limp, crawl, hobble—and in some cases even be carried—toward potential salvation. In the meantime, those around them would watch, jealously, as they continued to wait. But what became of those who left?

People would mistake him for a doctor when he was only a nurse. He tried to avoid the gazes that stuck to him like thorns.

As he was preparing to leave the hallway, he received a plea that he couldn't turn away from.

A woman had sprung before him, out of nowhere. She must have been fifty years old and her face was scarred by fatigue and suffering. Her thinness struck him: her arms, peeking through a camisole slung askew over her bony shoulders. They looked like the branches of a dead tree. Those were the arms that gripped Alioune's collar with undeniable strength. He stopped, surprised. The woman immediately fell to her knees and spoke, her voice whimpering.

"Doctor, doctor . . . My child, there . . ."

She indicated with her index finger a small child who was probably not even ten years old, lying on his back between two motionless bodies. He was wearing old khaki underwear and patched up sandals. His bare stomach was bloated and protruding, making him look somewhat ridiculous. His bent legs were covered in scars, some of them still bleeding. He had a white bandage on his head with a spot of blood on his forehead. He seemed to be asleep or unconscious, Alioune couldn't tell.

"My child," continued the woman, "He's going to die! Please help me, doctor. He's going to die, he's going to die . . ."

"Calm down, ma'am. Your son won't die, I'm sure of it. I promise you."

"Help me, doctor. Take him with you . . . He was wounded yesterday in the fight, you know, the fight . . . Someone threw a rock at his head. He's already lost a lot of blood. They put this bandage on yesterday. But the wound reopened, we need to treat him properly, he needs to be hospitalized, taken care of, given proper food, because I can't do it anymore, doctor," she pleaded.

"You know that the hospital is only able to take in a very small number of people, the urgent cases."

"And my child is not an urgent case? Look at him! He might be dead. He fell asleep, I'm scared he won't wake up."

The woman, still kneeling and clutching Alioune's clothing, was now screaming angrily. The young man examined the child. His eyes became teary, then he looked at the mother.

"I'm sorry, ma'am, I can't do anything, I am not a doctor yet," said Alioune with his head lowered.

"But there are no doctors here! Who here is a doctor? Please . . . Please have pity on my child. He's all I have in this world. Who here is a doctor?"

Amid the resounding indifference, the mother burst into tears.

"Ma'am," said Alioune calmly.

But the woman was still not reacting. Her tears could be heard from one end of the corridor to the other.

"Someone shut this woman up, what the hell! We've had enough of your cries all day long. We're sick too. Why should your son's case get priority?" Someone in the crowd yelled.

Alioune didn't turn around. It would have been pointless.

"I'm going to see what I can do, ma'am . . ."

"No! No, doctor! Don't tell me, 'I'll see what I can do.' All of your colleagues say that. Don't tell me that. Help me, I beg of you. Don't leave me alone . . ."

At that moment, the child woke up, disoriented, and could not see his mother: he was looking for her frantically. She was exhausted and couldn't move. She collapsed and began to groan softly. The child recognized her voice and ran toward her. He lifted his eyes toward Alioune with a strange look, almost menacing, then leaned toward his crying mother.

"Mom, Mom, I'm awake, wake up! It hurts. Mom!"

Upon hearing these words, Alioune removed himself silently and continued walking. He had just decided that he would personally take care of this mother and her child. Theoretically, he had neither the right nor the expertise. But did that even matter in such circumstances? At this point, it was just about helping people to the best of one's abilities. At nineteen years of age, Alioune was forced to become fifty.

Nevertheless, before going back to the mother and her child, he decided to go and see his friend Malamine. He headed toward the intensive care unit where the doctor had been locked up for almost two days.

CHAPTER 16

M alamine had been sitting still at the bedside for four hours, watching his wife sleep. Ndey Joor had finally arrived at the hospital at dawn. She had had nightmares, become delirious, and had yelled constantly throughout the night. This was the result of her fever and the many tranquilizers and anesthetics which Malamine had administered to help heal her wounds. Malamine couldn't sleep, despite the exhaustion that ensued from being on watch for two full days and performing all kinds of surgeries. His anxiety was too great, his nerves too tense, and his sadness too deep.

Around the same time the previous day, around 2 P.M., he received the news. He was in the middle of performing surgery on a patient whose wound, resulting from an amputation, had become infected and was threatening the poor guy with septicemia. Regardless of the fatigue that clouded his thoughts, Malamine could still remember: Madjigueen Ngoné had come bursting into the operating wing. She forced him to interrupt his work, to look at her. For the first time since he'd met her, she looked angry. He remembered the few words they exchanged clearly:

"What's gotten into you, Madjigueen?"

"I'm sorry, Malamine, I didn't want to interrupt you, but I couldn't avoid it. It's an emergency."

"There are nothing but emergencies here, you know that . . ."

"Malamine, I would have never allowed myself to come in

like this if it wasn't extremely important," Madjigueen Ngoné replied, with urgency in her voice. "There is a woman in the hallway. She's unconscious. The boy that she's with told me that he's your son, and that the wounded woman is his mother, your wife. She was beaten by the soldiers and is losing a lot of blood. You need to come."

The young woman then left the room. For a few seconds, Malamine was completely absent. He seemed to have misunderstood what Madjigueen just told him. He stayed like this, paralyzed, without saying a word, his mouth open, arms dangling. Then, suddenly, as if jolted by an electric shock, he came back from the dead, dropped the scalpel in his right hand, and turned to face the four men assisting him.

"Take over, Mr. Diakité," he said to one of them. "I trust you, you can do it without me. You've seen me do it hundreds of times."

He said this calmly before leaving the room.

Ndey Joor was becoming restless in her sleep: she whispered something, then calmed down. Malamine grabbed the fan on the bedside table which he used to ward off the flies attracted to Ndey Joor's exposed wounds. He wasn't able to bandage them because there were too many, and they were too deep. He feared that in this heat, a bandage would only infect and irritate them further. He was fanning his wife's body, but couldn't bring himself to look at her lacerated back. No, he didn't have the courage. He looked at her face; it finally seemed restful.

He put the fan down.

He could see Ndey Joor Camara's inanimate body among the other sick and wounded people. It looked like a cloth soaked in blood.

And her back . . .

Torn apart. Cut open. Bloody. Four deep wounds covered her back in all their horror, from her shoulder blades all the way down to her lower back. Her skin, which was once a pure black, was now bloody. At first, he didn't know what to do: he was still, his trembling hands hovered over her exposed back, unsure of how to touch it. Tears involuntarily fell onto his cheeks. He glanced at those around him—people he didn't recognize—with a pleading look in his eyes. He just wanted help, any help. The sick people around him didn't move. They watched, without much emotion or empathy, as tears rolled down his cheeks. Then, slowly, he began to recognize the faces. He saw Alioune kneeling in front of him on the other side of his wife's body, telling him things that, at first, he couldn't understand. He saw Madjigueen Ngoné preparing a stretcher next to him. Then, a few feet away, he saw his two children. Idrissa was keeping Rokaya, who was in tears, from getting too close. He saw their eyes overtaken by the same fear and confusion that he felt. His eyes met Idrissa's. They were gaunt and frightened, but also filled with anger. Anger toward him. He wanted to go and hug his son, reassure him and ask for his forgiveness. But there was no time: his wife was losing blood and he had to save her. He turned away from his children and helped two nurses lift the body, facedown, onto the stretcher. Thinking back on it, he remembered Alioune followed by two other men, lifting the stretcher and heading toward the intensive care unit. He remembered a dislocated arm dangling from the stretcher. He then hurried toward his crying kids to ask them if they had also been hurt. Rokhaya had a small wound on her hand. She was screaming.

"Save Mom," responded Idrissa, sharply. "I'll take care of Rokhy."

He didn't respond, but asked Madjigueen Ngoné to take care of them before he left.

Then, without turning around, he ran to save Ndey Joor Camara.

Someone was knocking on the door.

"Come in," he said.

Alioune appeared with a small bag in his hand.

"Oh, it's you . . ."

"How is she?"

"She's stable. She fell asleep at dawn. She was delirious all night, despite what I gave her. She was crying, screaming the name of our daughter Rokhaya, and wouldn't stop saying 'no.' I tried to talk to her, but she couldn't hear me. Everything she was saying seemed to be the result of the delirium caused by the fever. She hasn't opened her eyes. I'm relieved she's calmed down."

Malamine's voice was weak and exhausted. Alioune could tell his friend hadn't slept in two nights.

"You're exhausted, Malamine. Let me cover for you."

"Thank you. But I intend to care for her. I want to be there when she opens her eyes."

"As you wish, I understand."

Ndey Joor Camara was stretched out on her stomach, her back exposed to the air. Alioune stared at the deep wounds caused by the whip. He could sense the brutality of what had happened from the depth and size of the wounds alone.

"I brought you something to eat," continued Alioune. "I'm sure you haven't even thought about eating since yesterday. Here."

"Thank you, put that there," answered Malamine. "I'm not hungry, but Ndey Joor will be hungry when she wakes up. I'll give it to her."

The young nurse understood and realized it was useless to say anything more. He was about to leave when Malamine, without looking at him, called his name.

"Yes?" asked Alioune.

"Thank you so much."

"You're welcome."

Both were silent for a moment.

"I wanted to tell you, Malamine," continued Alioune.

He was silent again, as if he had lost his words or was looking for a better way to express them. Malamine stayed in the same position, looking away.

"I wanted to tell you," continued Alioune, "that you're not responsible for all this. You shouldn't feel guilty for what happened. I know it's easy for me, from where I'm standing, to tell you this, but we have a tendency to feel guilty as soon as any misfortune happens around us. So I wanted to tell you . . . Please. You were doing your job, and . . . Well . . ."

Alioune went quiet once again, unable to finish his sentence. He would have wanted to say all of this more calmly, delicately, with more empathy.

"Alioune, I don't feel responsible or guilty. I feel powerless. It's worse. What's the point of fighting?"

"Malamine, you have no right . . ."

"I have no right? I have no right?" Malamine stood up, knocking down the chair he was sitting on; he was yelling. "I have no right, you say? Look at my wife! Look at her!"

In a sudden gesture and without looking, he pointed his index finger toward Ndey Joor.

"Look at her back and tell me again, straight into my eyes, that I have no right to feel powerless. Who has the right, then? Who could possibly be more entitled to that right? All of you speak like books, you, Déthié, and the others . . ."

"Malamine, you . . ."

"Quiet! Shut up! This isn't going anywhere! Do you understand? Nowhere? I don't know what got into me for believing that we could defeat this madness. I don't remember anything from the lessons that those people taught me in the past. There's nothing we can do to fight all of this! Nothing!"

He was screaming angrily, unwittingly. Ndey Joor Camara, bothered by the noise, moved on the bed. She wanted to turn around to lie on her wounded back but Malamine, in a state of panic, stopped her and turned her back onto her stomach.

Silence fell back upon the small room. Malamine was panting. He stood up and lowered his head toward his wife, who was now peacefully asleep. He may have been crying silently.

"I'm going to get you another meal," Alioune said calmly. "You need to eat. Keep the one I gave you for your wife, if you like, but you need to eat. I'll be back."

Alioune opened the door.

"Alioune, I . . ."

"I'm not mad at you."

Then he left the room. As he was getting further away, he thought he heard Malamine bursting into tears.

CHAPTER 17

Once the fatigue caught up with him, Malamine finally fell asleep.

The depression that followed his sudden bout of anger was so intense that he fell into a deep sleep immediately after eating the meal that Alioune had brought him. Once he opened his eyes and escaped the dreamlike state that follows every deep slumber, he noticed his wife, looking at him. Although it was getting dark, a soft twilight allowed him to see everything clearly. Ndey Joor Camara was staring at him, smiling.

"You're always so handsome when you sleep, Malamine. I've been looking at you for an hour. You seem so tired. I heard you talking in your sleep."

"Ndey Joor, how . . ." mumbled Malamine.

That was all he managed to say. His throat tightened, perhaps because his emotions got the best of him, or perhaps because his ideas were not yet clear enough to express them coherently.

"I'm okay, I feel better," continued Ndey Joor Camara. "I think I slept for a long time. Malamine . . ."

Her voice grew worried.

"Yes, Ndey Joor . . ."

"How is Rokhaya? Where is she? What happened to her? And Idrissa? His voice was the last thing that I heard before . . ."

"Don't speak too much, Ndey Joor, the kids are alright.

Rokhaya just has a small cut on her hand. Idrissa is well. He's the one who brought you here. I left them with a colleague of mine. They're at her place now."

"Did they eat? Why did you leave them? You should've stayed with them, I'm sure they need you and . . ."

He interrupted her.

"You needed me, too. I couldn't leave you. The kids are in good hands."

His deep and reassuring voice calmed Ndey Joor Camara. She closed her eyes for a bit, as if about to fall asleep again.

"How are you, Malamine?" she said as she opened them again. "I haven't seen you in two days. You must be exhausted."

"I'm used to it, you know that. But you, Ndey Joor, how are you doing? I was so scared . . ."

"I feel a bit heavy and stiff. But I'm alright, I don't really feel any pain, but the area where my skin was ripped apart feels itchy."

She paused, as if trying to remember what had happened. Malamine said nothing.

"I guess it's not very pretty to look at," she finally added.

"Ndey Joor, I'm sorry . . . I should have been there . . . I . . ."

"Malamine, look at me," she interrupted.

He lifted his head, and she noticed he had tears in his eyes.

"Listen to me carefully, Malamine," continued Ndey Joor Camara. "For once, listen carefully."

She told him beautiful things, things about his guilt, which she thought was absurd. She reminded him that she admired him for everything he was and all the things he did. Malamine tried to interrupt, but what she said was so touching that he couldn't help but listen, even though the guilt was tearing him apart. Suddenly, he realized that like everybody else, he also needed to be reassured, to be told that he was not to blame.

He felt a bit ashamed for having such a basic need, but Ndey Joor's words calmed him. She told him that she was proud of having said no in her own way, without going against the values that they shared. She told him that if she were to do it over again, she would do it all the same because he was taking risks, too. Finally, she told him that she loved him with all her heart.

By the time she stopped speaking, the room had been plunged into a deep and peaceful darkness. The outlines of the objects became vague. The noises of the day faded, one after the other.

Ndey Joor seemed to be struggling to catch her breath after speaking. Malamine could no longer see her but sensed her quickening breath. A feeling of shame overwhelmed him. He turned on the bedside table lamp. A soft yellow light filled the room. He looked for his wife's eyes, but she had turned around.

"They told me what happened yesterday. You were great," he said.

She turned toward him. Her face was covered in tears, but she was smiling. She held out her hand. He grabbed it. They stayed like this for a few long minutes.

"What happened yesterday, after I fainted?"

Without omitting any details, he recounted the previous night's events. He had only learned of them a few hours prior, when Alioune came back with his meal. Once he finished, Ndey Joor sighed and felt a hint of bitterness emerge in her.

"So, the people who'd gathered around intervened. I hope there won't be any retaliation against them, against you, or against the kids because of me. I really hope so. These people are so crazy! They're capable of anything. Anything at all. I wouldn't want them to take me again . . . Not after . . ."

Suddenly overtaken by her emotions, her voice cracked.

"Now's not the time to talk about all this, Ndey Joor. You need to rest. That's what you really need. Until you come home, I'm going to take care of you and the kids."

For the first time in a long time, Malamine smiled.

CHAPTER 18

I'm sorry I didn't write to you sooner.
I couldn't bring myself to do it. Physically, I couldn't
bring myself to do it. I was beaten, my husband beat
me. Usually, I pick myself back up without too much difficulty because I learned to cheat, to wail at the top of my
lungs to calm his fury. There are even days when he stops
beating me after only a few blows, because he thinks I'm on
the verge of fainting. I've endured this for twenty-five years.
Usually, I recover. But this time, he hit me hard, and for a
long time. I screamed, I pleaded, I cried, but nothing
stopped him. He hit, hit, hit, hit, and hit me again. He hit
me until the hitting and slapping brought me to the ground.
Until I was motionless, almost dead. I broke an arm when
I fell, my right eye is swollen, and I lost two teeth. My body
hurts: the slightest movement is painful. You may have
noticed that my handwriting is different than it was in my
first letter: my arms are in a cast, so I asked my neighbor's
daughter to write this letter for me. I won't make it long, as
I don't want to tire her too much. I'll make up for it once
I'm better, I promise.

Aïssata, he hit me hard, as if he didn't know me, as if he
was drunk. As if he was drunk . . .

He hit me because I disagreed with him. Because I stood
up to him. Because I said no. It was about our son. He said
that his body was going to be thrown into the desert, into that
dump where they throw the people they execute: murderers,

tiaga,[21] *men and women who have committed adultery. I refused, because my son is not a dog. I wanted him to have a grave, just like your daughter, a grave where I could mourn and cry. But my husband refused. He said Lamine was a dog, a son of a bitch who deserved everything that happened to him and who would go burn in hell. I refused to accept that he would be thrown into the desert, I swear I refused with all of my strength. He asked me to be quiet, I refused, and then he hit me.*

When I was almost unconscious and my neighbors were taking care of me, he left without a word, without looking at me. I was told he went out to follow the car that drove our son to the communal dump . . . He won't have a grave. I won't have a grave to celebrate his memory or to go to and cry. No sign with his name. He disappeared. Who will remember him in ten years? Who will remember Lamine Kanté? Without a grave, he will be forgotten . . . My heart will be his grave, my memory his coffin, my soul his cemetery. But when I die, when I reunite with him, who will remember Lamine Kanté? Who will say that he loved your daughter? Who will remember that he was twenty years old? Without a grave, he died twice, Aïssata . . .

I thought a lot about the story that you told me, of that woman beaten in the street. I feel like she and I are the same: she was also beaten when she said no . . .

The crowd's reaction, Aïssata, I don't know how to explain it, but I have a piece of advice for you: don't look for the causes of our children's death. There is only one and you know it: madness. It's the only true reason. But we must stay out of all this, Aïssata. Let your pain take you above all this. You can't change the course of history. Suffer, suffer. But

[21] Prostitutes.

suffer like a queen. Suffer like a mother. Remove yourself from the world. You're alone, nobody understands you, nobody wants to understand you, nobody can understand you. Collapse alone. Break down alone. Don't look at the world, it doesn't understand you and you cannot understand it.

I'm going to stop the letter here and let my temporary secretary go. I will write to you again soon, I promise. I miss you.

Sadobo

S itting alone in the back of the pickup truck that was moving slowly toward the hospital, Abdel Karim watched, stone-faced, as Kalep's barren landscape unfolded.

He was proud of all they had been able to accomplish in Kalep. When they first took over four years ago, the city was dirty, corrupt, possessed by the Devil, abandoned by God. The city was becoming increasingly lecherous in the name of modernity. Abdel Karim's heart still shuddered at the thought of the scene that had greeted them when they arrived: women dressed indecently like westerners, their heads bare, breasts almost exposed, shoulders uncovered, stomachs revealing the navel and the demonic outline of their kidneys, buttocks tightly molded into skinny jeans which were obviously too tight. An array of hedonistic distractions were turning Muslims away from the Voice of the Lord: bistros, bars, nightclubs—barely disguised whorehouses where the sinful masses of Kalep's youth would come to destroy, debase, and damn themselves. The Devil used these weapons to keep people clenched in his iron fist. People were consumed by material pleasures and led sinful lives. This overindulgence was everywhere: in cybercafes, where people actively participated in their own damnation through a screen; in hair salons, where women trimmed and dyed their hair to better seduce men; and finally, in all of the behaviors that went against Islam and made up the day-to-day life of Kalep's people: music, dance, and iconography. That's what they encountered when they first arrived in

Kalep. They became the shepherds of a herd of lost and damned souls who needed to be brought back to the sacred prairies of the Lord's chosen sheep. It took them four years, four long years during which they encountered a fair share of hostility and distrust. That didn't worry Abdel Karim: the Devil's only weapon is the deceitful darkness into which he plunges those who succumb to him; to fight against him is to shine God's light into the darkened hearts of these men.

That was their mission. They made it their divine vocation. They persisted and fought against Satan. After a certain amount of time, the people came to understand that the Brotherhood was working toward their salvation. Slowly, the people's hostility began to dissipate. It was replaced by fear. God returned to Kalep.

And it was he, Abdel Karim, who played such a large part in bringing Him back.

As he remembered this, he smiled. But not a smile of satisfaction or blissful self-glorification; it was a humble smile, those that come involuntarily to certain people. People who are filled with overwhelming joy from the contemplation of an idea greater than themselves, from a feeling they couldn't get anywhere else.

Abdel Karim was governed by the idea of Duty.

The French speak of a "man of duty" and a "heightened sense of duty." As nice and powerful as these expressions may be, they don't really apply to Abdel Karim as we know him. And while they might've flattered the common man, they would have also robbed someone like Abdel Karim of his splendor. Abdel Karim was anything but a common man. He wasn't a man of duty; he was Duty, its embodiment; he didn't *have* a duty, he *was* Duty in the flesh. Two verbs applied to his tyrannical idea of duty: to serve and to punish. All of his actions, his thoughts, his entire life, tended toward these two imperatives: Service and Punishment.

And to serve what? The religion and those who serve it.

And to punish whom? Those who do not serve the religion or belittle it.

And in the name of what? Duty.

And toward whom? God.

That's how this man reasoned. One must nonetheless be wary of judging him too hastily. Behind these terse and rival assumptions hid a sharp mind and a mysterious personality. Abdel Karim Konaté wasn't one of those dogmatists whose unreasonable, limited logic was only as powerful as the idiotic exaltation with which it was preached. He wasn't one of those middle of the road Muslim fanatics whose thinking was impartial, arbitrary, or authoritarian, founded on a literal interpretation of the Quran, stripped from any real theoretical and philosophical reflection. He didn't choose to serve the Fundamental Law through imitation or because somebody had forced him to, but because he had reflected deeply on the matter, and from his lengthy meditation he had discovered the following truth: the Fundamental Law is the only law which reflects not only the letter of the Quran, but also its spirit.

He had joined the Brotherhood a long time ago. His father had died serving it. His mother, grief-stricken, could not outlive his father and died in his arms a few months later. An only child, Abdel Karim hadn't wished to live with an uncle, as had been suggested to him. He'd quit his theological studies and joined the Brotherhood. This happened around the time that the Brotherhood was still in its early stages. Its members were hiding in the desert, preparing a big crusade, one which, after several years and many battles, is what allowed them to access Sumal, to take over Kalep and eventually Bandiani. Abdel Karim joined the Brotherhood for the same reasons he had decided to study theology: to truly understand what it means to be a Muslim. Over a few years, theology had taught him the theory. The Brotherhood would teach him the practice. That's what he had thought, and so he enrolled. He was eighteen years old at the time. Now, he was thirty-seven. Through his calm demeanor, his unwavering dedication, courage, deep knowledge of the religious text, his faithfulness, his exemplary character in combat and in his service to God, he worked his way to the top of the Brotherhood's hierarchy. He first became lieutenant, then captain, and finally five years ago, chief of the Islamic police.

This man was the incarnation of fanaticism in its most dangerous form: he was an intelligent fanatic, if those terms can even be rightfully juxtaposed. He was a fanatic capable of conveying his thoughts through clear argumentation. And, like all great fanatics, he was unwavering in his convictions. Impassioned fanatics are the least dangerous: their own foolishness, which they're not even conscious of, is enough to condemn them; it reduces them to the sad and tragic dimension of poor minstrels. But reserved fanatics, those whose enthusiasm manifests only in their overwhelmingly calm demeanor and in the precision of their gestures, these are the ones to be feared. Real fanaticism finds its most authentic and dangerous expression in the elites who embody it: in those educated, at least partly, in western schools, in those who master rhetoric, who grasp its subtleties, who understand its language and know how to use it skillfully.

Abdel Karim was one of those.

He read the Quran, studied it: he discovered the very essence of this religion. He didn't believe in the existence of multiple Islams. That seemed profane to him. Was there not just one God? Was he not taught the singularity of the Lord? What could be the significance of two Islams, if not the very negation of this singularity? Before joining the Brotherhood, Abdel Karim had been aware of both Islams. They were strangely different: one was radical Islam, the other moderate Islam. At the time, he told himself that one of the two had to be false. He believed that one of them must simply be a means to justify negligence with respect to divine scripture, all while using the idea of God and the Word of the Quran in order to do so. He knew that one of these two supposed Islams was false. Initially, he didn't know which one. So he waited. He observed. He reflected. Then, with time, he realized that moderate Islam was extraordinarily silent. Its allegiance and credibility were not founded on any action, as if it were enough to simply announce that one believes in God as sufficient proof of one's faith. He recognized that radical Islam had given birth to the moderate one, that the latter defined itself only in contrast to the former. Moderate Islam was but a failed attempt to legitimize that which could not be: a fanciful, over-simplified, fantasized interpretation of the Quran as a means of aligning religion with outside ideas, ideas which are simply incompatible with the Word of the Book. Radical Islam was founded on actions. Sometimes violent, yes. Sometimes abrupt, yes. Sometimes bloody, yes. But all done in the name of the Lord, always done in His Name, with His Blessing, under His Eyes.

That's why he joined the Brotherhood.

He had no regrets. Today, almost twenty years after his decision to join the Brotherhood, radical Islam was growing. It could be heard and seen, it made no concessions, and it was spreading. The Islam that he chose was winning the battle and taking over the field. The other Islam stumbled on its own contradictions; it stuttered, it was incapable of putting forth a clear line of thought, of following a clear path in the face of an unholy alternative: deceive God or deceive the West. It was unable to give a coherent interpretation of exactly what this religion was. He laughed whenever he came across a western radio station discussing the idea of a secular, tolerant, and democratic Islam. This Islam had been built, distorted, manipulated, and became mainstream through the utterance of ungodly things, and Abdel Karim hated it. An Islam that tries to open itself to the world will necessarily fail, and what was known as moderate Islam was an adequate reflection of this failure. Islam, or so he thought, would not tolerate any political graft without risking its own demise. Moderate Islam failed to stand behind a logical set of principles, which validated Abdel Karim's faith toward the radical one, the real one, the only one. Abdel Karim was certain that radical Islam would soon win in the face of a lazy Islam. The latter merely claims to be moderate, but in reality its followers fear their own religion. That was its biggest failure, according to Abdel Karim; it was the greatest defiance against God. He was convinced that soon, the Brotherhood and all its radical groups would come together and rally Muslims all around the world. Their perseverance would pay off.

Kalep was a strategic stronghold, irreplaceable in the Brotherhood's fight against Sumal's army. Occupying Kalep meant controlling not only the north of the country whose riches, resources, and tourism made up half of the country's national GDP, but it also meant controlling the northern front, the road in the desert, thus facilitating the troops' access to vital resources, and training. Abdel Karim was glad they had taken this city, and under no circumstance would they abandon it to the enemy, even if it meant losing. So long as he lived, Kalep would not be handed over to the enemy. Abdel Karim had given his word to God and El Hadj Majidh, one of the Fraternity's great qadis, who was in charge of the organization's troops in that part of the country. He had raised this city, shaped it, rebuilt it. He'd given it a new face, a real, respectable, and honorable one. This garrison was all his.

The pickup truck began to slow down. Abdel Karim emerged from his thoughts and paid closer attention to what was happening outside. They arrived at the hospital.

* * *

Alioune and Malamine stood upright; their demeanor was serious and they stared back at the giant without batting an eyelid. He had just made his way into their room and was looking back and forth at both of them. Ndey Joor Camara was sitting on the bed. Her head was covered with a black veil and she was dressed in a lightweight camisole through which peeked the faint outline of her bandages. Her face reflected a serenity which contrasted starkly with the quasi-hostile somberness of the three men who were with her.

Abdel Karim had given no advance notice of his visit. Malamine and Alioune were surprised when the door opened on the enormous figure of the head of Kalep's Islamic police. Both men recognized him immediately and stood up abruptly when he entered. They watched him without saying a word.

Abdel Karim could instantly feel that both men were not fond of him, despite their reserved and calm attitudes. But he wasn't there for a confrontation and quickly overlooked the silent yet quite perceptible animosity being directed at him. He glanced over quickly at the woman on the bed. She was the one he came to see. Her face was beautiful, with delicate features and a complexion of the purest black. Abdel Karim became unsettled for a moment in the face of her unwavering tranquility—did she even notice him? She didn't seem surprised like the two men were. Her expression was graced with nothing but serenity. After a few seconds, he decided to interrupt this silence.

"*Assalamu Aleïkum.* I am Captain Abdel Karim Konaté, chief of Kalep's police. Is this where *Adjaratou* Ndey Joor Camara was admitted?"

"Yes, that's her," answered Malamine. "To what do we owe the honor of your visit, Captain? Is there a problem?"

"May I ask who you are, *El Hadj*?"

"Doctor Malamine Camara. I'm this woman's husband. And this is Alioune Diop, the nurse."

Malamine's voice was blunt. At no point did he turn his eyes away from his interlocutor's powerful gaze, which was trying to destabilize him. There was now a duel between the men.

"Are you the one caring for your wife, Doctor Camara?"

"Of course, Captain."

"How is she doing?"

"Her wounds are healing slowly, but she must remain here a few more days. The gashes that your men gave her are very deep and will need time to close up again."

He had insisted on "*your men*." At that moment, Alioune looked over at the captain. He did not bat an eyelid. Alioune was unsure whether he should feel satisfied or afraid. Malamine was struggling to conceal his animosity. His face was serious, somber, and his lower lip twitching slightly. Alioune knew this was a sign of extreme nervousness.

"How much longer do you think she'll need before she can leave, doctor?"

"I don't know. She needs rest, not only physical rest, but also emotional rest. But you still haven't told us what brings you here today, Captain. What do you want from my wife?"

"To present to her, and to you as well since you are here, the Brotherhood's apologies. I was informed of what happened. My men," Alioune noticed a slight change in his tone when he pronounced these two words, "had, from the Sharia perspective, absolutely no right to beat this woman. They should have asked her to cover herself and left it at that. But under no circumstance should they have lifted a hand to her. It's not written anywhere in the Quran. This is an unfortunate incident which we all regret. This is why I came: to apologize, on behalf of the Brotherhood. And on my own behalf as well."

"Thank you, Captain," responded Malamine. "Will that be all?"

"No, doctor."

"Oh?"

The giant took his eyes off Malamine and fixed his gaze on Ndey Joor Camara. She hadn't moved since he entered the room. Her expression remained unchanged. He looked at her for a long time, without saying a word.

"Captain?"

"I came to ask the unfairly beaten victim what fate she wishes for those who beat her."

He didn't take his eyes off Ndey Joor.

"Excuse me, Captain? I'm afraid I don't fully understand what you are asking my wife."

"I'm going to repeat myself, doctor, if you'd like. But I ask that your wife be the only person to answer and make the decision. The men who beat you, ma'am, had no right to do so. In the light of our Law, they have committed an offense. This same Law punishes those who are responsible for injustice, especially when they commit these injustices under the false pretext that they are done in the service of God. As a result, they must be punished."

"Very well, Captain, but I still don't understand how my wife is involved here. Punish them according to the laws you obey."

"The problem, doctor," said the captain, who was now turning again toward Malamine, "is that the only possible punishment is one that is chosen by the victim. Or by his or her family, if the victim has died. And since, in this case, your, wife *survived*," he said this without a shudder, "it is up to her to decide the fate of her tormentors."

"With all due respect, Captain . . ."

"With all due respect, doctor, I'd like to hear only from your wife."

Malamine, whose face had tensed, was about to respond when his wife interrupted him.

"Don't worry, Malamine . . ."

Then she looked at the giant, whose gaze was fixed on her.

"Captain," she began . . .

"Ma'am."

"I thank you for your apologies. As for your request, I don't think I can accept, Captain."

"What do you mean?"

"I mean that I refuse to choose a punishment. Do with these men what you like. They are your men, after all."

"Allow me to insist. If you do not choose, we will cut their hands off."

"Then do nothing, Captain. I forgive them, let them be. I am under the impression that they have already received a severe enough punishment."

"I don't doubt the generosity of your soul, ma'am, but that's not possible."

"Why not?"

"It's not fair."

"Do you know what's fair and what isn't?"

"I claim that I do, Adja. I know what justice is. Or, at the very least, what it isn't. And what it isn't is leaving those in error immune from punishment. With the help of justice, the offended party makes the offender pay, otherwise this world would merely be survival of the fittest."

"That's not the idea I have of justice, Captain. It's neither revenge nor the law of talion. Allow *me* to insist. Do as you like."

"As you wish. We will cut off their hands in two days, in public. You can come witness the punishment," answered Abdel Karim.

"Given my current state, I'm afraid that will be difficult. And besides, it's not important to me."

"Very well, I respect your decision. I won't bother you any further. I wish you a quick recovery, *in Sha Allah. Assalamu Aleïkum.*"

He took a few steps toward the door, pretending not to pay attention to both men in the room. Then he stopped, his hand on the doorknob. He turned around, gave Ndey Joor a strange look, then murmured something gently, but still loudly enough for all to hear: "You remind me of someone, ma'am."

And before anyone could answer, he was gone. Alioune looked over at Malamine and noticed he was shaking.

What they did a few days ago proves they're insane! Insane! Cutting off the hands of three of their own men! They shy away from nothing and would kill their own mothers in the name of their God if they had to. We can't wait any longer, we have to publish this journal!"

"Publish! It would be suicidal to rush it, you know that."

"Yes, publish! I don't know what's holding all of you back. Are you scared? I say we need to respond immediately, show them that we're not afraid of them. Let's publish the journal tomorrow, it's almost ready!"

"Don't be in such a hurry, Déthié. You know very well that this shouldn't be done out of fear, but with patience and reflection. I think we should include this incident."

"But why, Codou? It was staged . . ."

"Exactly, to expose the sham, to speak of it ironically."

Déthié opened his mouth to reply when Alioune interrupted.

"I'd like to say a word. I was there, I took photos. I got a really strange feeling, actually, behind the lens. Like Déthié, I'm not so sure that this execution was simply a strategic way to send a message. I mean, yes, but not only that . . . there was something very real in what was happening. I mean, something that wasn't fake or staged, that wasn't acted. It wasn't just a farce. There was a real desire for justice. It wasn't just an act."

"What you're saying, Alioune, isn't so different from what I'm saying," continued Déthié. "What these men have enacted is their madness. It's a demonstration of power . . . But you still haven't answered, except you, Codou. Do we publish this journal now, or not?"

"Personally, I think that we should wait a bit, be patient. This thing that we've been working on for all of these months must be successful. And in order for it to be successful, it can't be rushed. We must wait for the best occasion, for the most favorable circumstances. If they catch us, we're dead, good for a public execution."

It was Vieux Faye who had spoken.

"And why do you think the circumstances aren't favorable?"

Vieux Faye cleared his throat like a great orator seeking to move his audience. His jaw was moving frantically as he chewed his gum, and he began his speech.

"The images of the mutilation you spoke of earlier have made their way all over the province: even in Soro people were talking about it. We can't forget the real reason for this gesture. Officially, it was meant to punish those who beat your wife, Malamine. But in truth, I believe the real reason for this mutilation was to reinstate a power that had become unstable. Don't forget that the only reason Ndey Joor is still alive is because people from the crowd saved her life. I'm not sure if you recognize the power of this prohibited act: it's the first time since the Brotherhood took control of the province that it has had to encounter the people's opposition. It's exceptional!"

"We know that, Vieux Faye," Déthié spoke. "You wrote an article on this very topic, which we all found brilliant. But that still doesn't explain why the circumstances aren't favorable to publish this journal. On the contrary, I think that the indignation that has blown over Kalep works to our advantage. We could use it in our favor to rally all of those who are scared."

"Almost everyone is scared."

"Yes, exactly, everyone is scared. We could convince them to fight back. In my opinion, there is no circumstance more favorable, my friends. I really don't see where you're trying to go with this, Vieux Faye, I . . ."

"I think I know where he's trying to go with this," interrupted Madjigueen. "The act of rebellion that saved Malamine's wife had a strong impact: it reinforced surveillance in the cities. In the last few days, patrols have multiplied. They're increasingly present. You can't walk for two minutes in Kalep without seeing one, and heavily armed militia are taking pleasure in searching people, especially women. The Brotherhood has become wary of the people, because it knows the people can retaliate against it. To attempt the distribution of an underground journal that encourages resistance is too risky right now."

"But Madjigueen, you too, Vieux Faye, and you, Codou," continued Déthié, whose voice was growing increasingly agitated. "There will never really be a perfect moment, because the Brotherhood is like a monster, projecting and inflicting terror over the people. This shadow will never disappear, you must convince yourself of that. What would you prefer? To wait it out even longer? Do you know what they'll do in the meantime? They'll kill others. They'll beat others. They'll mutilate others. Maybe even one of your own. We've seen that no one is safe. Next time, it might even be one of us. To wait out of fear is to let that fear defeat us without having fought the battle. Why wait when we know they will keep killing? We've already waited too long. I repeat: we have to take advantage of this wave of public outrage."

"You have too much faith in the people, Déthié," said Madjigueen Ngoné.

"Does that mean we should suspect them and make them our enemy?"

"Let's not forget that for all these years, the people have

been allies of the Brotherhood. Maybe they still are. We don't know what pushed them to fight back. These people have killed in the past, they've been silent, accomplices."

"But in our silence, we've all been accomplices at one point or another," protested Déthié. "Each and every one of us. We've all been witnesses and done nothing, said nothing. It took one of us, perhaps the bravest, to come forward and decide to act. But before that? We were all silent, too. Just like the others. We were also a part of the people. We still are."

"Except that we didn't kill. We have to be wary of large crowds, you never know whose side they're on, or what they will do."

"You're speaking like a nineteenth-century European aristocrat, Madjigueen, and that's disappointing coming from you. It's like you fear for your life or your possessions. You're not the one people will decide to attack, if they decide to attack."

Déthié was silent for a moment, then continued, looking at all of those present in the *Jambaar* with a look of solemn gravity on his face.

"You need to be convinced of one thing: our only ally is the people. Without them, there is no hope. Only the people can turn this barbaric situation around. It won't be us. This journal might, at best, give the people their hope back. I believe in the people despite what they have done. In any case, I have no choice. The people make up a dangerous and unpredictable entity. Perhaps. But one must never lose sight of the fact that this unpredictability can become an uncontrollable weapon. One day, they will fight back. And when that day comes, you'll be grateful. A populace gets beaten down, rises up again, suffers, but from enduring such suffering in silence it learns and it grows. The only ambition you're not allowed to have is the desire to be greater than the people. Don't fall for this trap, and never look down on what will always be greater than you, greater than all of us."

Déthié said these last words very softly, as if overcome by a sudden fatigue. His anger was either cold or had calmed down; he let himself fall into a chair, throwing his head back.

"If I speak like an aristocrat, you, Déthié, you speak like a dangerous ideologist, who considers the people to be a superior, almost mythical entity," answered Madjigueen. "You speak like a politician, like a hero, like a liar. People like you scare me: those who use the word 'people' without referring to singular persons, to individual destinies, to stories of suffering, but only to a single face, to a subject of thought. That scares me."

Déthié didn't answer.

A long silence followed. The only audible sound came from Père Badji, sitting away from the others, smoking his pipe. The room was small and poorly ventilated; the clouds of smoke remained suspended in the air, like blankets of fog. Alioune lit a cigarette and watched his own puffs of smoke rise toward the thick clouds which were spreading across the ceiling.

Every so often, they could hear the sound of a car, distant at first, then increasingly closer. The sound came from the depths of night, almost knocking on the doors of the room. Then the noise would grow faint again, melting into the evening's silence.

They were all quiet in the basement, each lost in thought. Another noise appeared shortly after and interrupted the silence. It was the voice of a man whose words were impossible to make out.

"What's that?" asked Vieux Faye, worried.

"It's Birame Penda, one of Kalep's homeless men," answered Madjigueen Ngoné. "I recognize his voice. He always sings at night."

"What's he singing?"

They listened. Initially, they understood nothing; then, slowly but surely, they were able to grasp the tune, a few words, an intonation. The words were unclear, poorly articulated, and the song was often interrupted by long silences, almost as if the singer had forgotten the lyrics. After some time, though, they recognized the majestic, deep, solemn words of "Niani."[22] Other voices emerged in the night and joined Birame Penda's. The homeless, crazy, *budjukat*,[23] the wounded, the *battù*,[24] and the marginalized, all the damned and forgotten people of Kalep had assembled somewhere not far off and were singing in unison. They created an enormous choir for Birame Penda whose voice became louder still, solitary, hoarse, far from beautiful but strong nonetheless. The tempo was sumptuously slow. The singers took their time, as if trying to grant this tune all of its epic power, its warrior qualities. The lyrics, which were isolated at first, rose from the singers' breasts and united in a single stream. Then their whispers and breath, still hot, lifted toward the sky.

They were there, lost somewhere in the night of a dark city, and their song echoed everywhere shamelessly. In the words and music that this great human voice poured over Kalep, one could almost hear the soft chords of a xalam,[25] the instrument that had originally accompanied this poem. Maybe it was God playing . . .

---

[22] In Senegal, "Niani" is a song of resistance to colonial occupation, dating from the nineteenth century. It was composed when Lat-Joor Ngoné Latir Joob (1842–1866), a Senegalese hero and famous king of the resistant province, was about to ask Maba Diaxu Ba (1809–1867), another great resistance fighter, to help him oppose the construction of a train which would cross both of their kingdoms, favor colonial expansion and domination, and threaten their independence. Today, "Niani" is used as a symbol of resistance to all forms of oppression.

[23] Individuals who, affected by misfortune, survive thanks to what they find, recycle, reuse, or sell in the dumps.

[24] In its literal sense, can be defined as a bowl. As metonymy, refers to the alms bowl's carrier, generally the beggar.

[25] A musical instrument with three cords (sometimes five), a handle, and an oval soundboard covered with cow or sheep skin: a West African lute, of sorts. It's played by most griots, including those who were present when "Niani" was first written.

This marvelous interlude lasted a mere five minutes before it was abruptly interrupted and morphed into fearful screams mingled with the sound of engines and gunshots.

The seven friends, startled, held their breath.

"We have to go out and help them!" said Déthié.

"No one can leave, it's too risky!" yelled Madjigueen Ngoné. "It always happens this way. Every time they sing, the militia comes and separates them. But they don't beat or kill them. They only fire to scare them off and force them to disperse. None of us can leave."

The commotion continued for a few minutes outside, then the stillness of the night prevailed again. The voice of Birame Penda fell silent.

In the basement of the *Jambaar*, calm returned, too. Each person was thinking and perhaps could still hear the tune of the poem which had burst forth into the sky before fading out.

Since the start of the meeting, Malamine Camara had spoken very little. He sat at the edge of a rectangular table with the others, motionless on his chair, arms crossed. An unvoiced anger had been building up inside him for a few days; he believed that the only way he could successfully conceal his bitterness was through silence. In the midst of this meeting fueled by tension, he had to keep calm. They had to make a decision.

"As far as the people are concerned, Déthié," he began after taking a deep breath, "I don't believe that Madjigueen looks down on them. I don't believe that anybody in this room could be more humble. I believe what she was trying to tell you is that these people won't let themselves be governed, not even by those who want to help them, because they're free and unpredictable."

"Especially not by *them*," whispered Vieux Faye.

"However," Malamine continued, "at one point or another, if they don't want to live in perpetual fear, they're going to have to fight back. Sooner rather than later. I don't know if we can contribute to the start of such an uprising. Truth be told, that's not what I'm looking to do. Such uprisings have more than just virtues. Ultimately, people can be free, but at what cost?"

"Yes, the brutalities of progress are called revolutions. When they are over, this fact is recognized,—that the human race has been treated harshly, but that it has progressed."[26]

A long silence welcomed these words pronounced by Déthié.

"It's Victor Hugo," he added a few seconds later, while the effect of the quote was still lingering.

"Our people are already being harshly treated, Déthié," answered Malamine. "But are they still moving forward despite this? No. They are crawling. Not like a snake ready to attack, but on all fours, like a wild animal, a man reduced to a beastly state. Let's try to prevent more blood from being shed. Too much blood has already been shed. I have no doubt Hugo would have agreed with me. What I would like . . ." he stopped to think for a few seconds, "yes, what I would like this journal to do," he continued, "is to bear witness. I would like it to show the people what they're being unknowingly subjected to. As for the publication date . . ."

He felt his anger rising, his impatience getting the better of him, his calmness fading. Six pairs of eyes faced him, all of them tense. The effects of the song had dissipated. Anxiety had returned.

"As for the publication date, I suggest we have a vote," Malamine concluded.

"You know very well that that's not what we agreed on," Déthié immediately responded.

"I know, I know. But it's too important to the group for me

---

[26] *Les Misérables*, Volume I, Book I, Chapter X (trans. Isabel F. Hapgood).

to decide alone. A vote seems like a reasonable compromise. Let's vote anonymously, and we'll see which side comes out victorious. That way, everyone will be able to give their opinion."

They voted. Each person wrote down their answer on a piece of paper which they then placed in a small container that Père Badji had gone to fetch from the bar.

"Let's have the youngest pick," said Malamine.

"Just a second, Alioune," said Codou. "What happens if it's a tie?"

"That's impossible: there are seven of us," Déthié answered his wife.

"But say one of us casts a blank vote . . ."

"Blank?"

"Anything is possible."

"Who would do that, and why? Come on, Codou . . ."

"We have to consider it."

"In that case," Malamine interrupted, "I'll make the final decision, if that's alright with you."

They accepted this suggestion. Alioune proceeded: there were three votes for "yes," three for "no," and one blank.

"Well, clearly the blank vote was a possibility! I'd be curious to know who cast it," said Déthié, staring at each of his friends one by one. "But what does it matter . . . My friend," he said turning toward Malamine with a big smile, "it seems that you've only delayed your responsibility. The gods want you to choose. We're all ears. Choose, let's get this done with."

Malamine straightened his back in his chair and took a deep breath. He had cast the blank vote to let his friends have the final say. Things had come back to him full circle. God had made him face his destiny. He hesitated, looked at each of his friends one after the other, lowered his head, then raised it again. His anger was bubbling inside him, and his efforts to keep it at bay were being dissipated by his inability to concentrate. He was hot. The fog from the smoke that still floated near the ceiling was making him short of breath. He had a headache. He wiped his forehead. As his anger rose, so did a feeling of weakness. He felt like giving up.

"Let's publish."

He wasn't sure whether this was really what he wanted to say. Déthié rejoiced.

Malamine lowered his head. He had been completely overwhelmed by anger and he was shaking. Two faces appeared before him. They mingled together, danced, converged, shrunk, grew, disappeared and reappeared like flames of fire in the wind: the face of the stoned woman who had said something before her death, and that of Abdel Karim.

CHAPTER 21

As Malamine made his way home, his watch showed that it was half past five in the morning. He was tired. The previous night's emotions had left him exhausted, and the exhaustion was only just beginning to catch up with him. They had worked all night.

They had agreed not to focus too much on the journal's aesthetic quality; truth be told, it didn't matter much at all. Simple sheets of paper in an A4 format, threaded together, would do the job. What mattered was whose hands the journal would fall into. They had agreed, after long and heated discussions, on a moderate-sized journal of thirty-two pages. He and Déthié, who had written the majority of the articles, would have preferred for it to be longer. As for Codou, Vieux Faye, and Madjigueen Ngoné, they were set on being concise, preferring to prioritize clarity over length. In the end, this was the more practical choice and would make the journal easier to read.

Some content had to be cut as a result of this decision. Articles had to be rewritten, some replaced altogether by summaries. Déthié was furious about this, but in the end, everything worked out.

One thousand seven hundred copies of the journal were stacked up in the *Jambaar*'s basement. Five hundred copies would be distributed to each of Bandiani's three main cities: Kalep, Bantika, and Soro, and two hundred for Akanté, a small conglomeration.

When it came time to finalize the layout, Madjigueen

Ngoné pointed out—to everyone's surprise—that the journal didn't have a name yet. In the minutes that followed, they discussed potential options: titles, puns, plays on words. Père Badji almost laughed.

Amid the hysterical laughter, Malamine had been forced to interrupt the banter. They really had to find a title. That's when Déthié suggested "Jambaar." Vieux Faye thought it was a nice idea, but might lead the Brotherhood back to the tavern. "As tempting as it might be, we shouldn't underestimate them," he added, which caused even more laughter.

"What about *Rambaaj*?" asked Codou, suddenly.

Initially, nobody reacted. Alioune spoke first:

"A perfect anagram of *Jambaar*, almost a palindrome. I think it's a great idea, Codou. Bravo."

Rambaaj. The approval was unanimous. Literally, this name referred to an evil, wicked spirit who eavesdrops behind closed doors, sparks trouble, breaks friendships and couples apart, and spreads chaos in the minds of others through lies and manipulation. But was this not, metaphorically and symbolically, exactly what they hoped to accomplish with this journal? To condemn the savagery and instill doubt in the minds of Bandiani's people? To be, in a way, *diabolos*,[27] hoping to *separate* the people from what's oppressing them? They would be *rambaaj* without the lies.

It was a subtle idea.

And so *Rambaaj* was born. They planned to meet again the following night. Each of them would take a batch of copies and begin the distribution.

Malamine went straight to his room, which was located on the ground floor next to the kitchen. Ndey Joor, who had left

[27] Greek word meaning "the separator," which later on acquired a religious connotation to refer to the Devil.

the hospital the day after Abdel Karim's visit, was most likely asleep on the upper floor, like the rest of the family. Upon entering the room, Malamine noticed a soft odor of incense floating around. This made for a hospitable and warm atmosphere; the tiredness that had tensed his body dissipated. *Curray*[28] invigorates the soul and relaxes the body before being an aphrodisiac for the senses: all those who think otherwise are mistaken. He turned on the small lamp on the nightstand and began to undress.

"Finally, you're here, Malamine. I was worried, you know."

"Ndey Joor . . ."

He must have woken her up. She was stretched out on her side—her bruises bothered her still—and was looking at him.

"I'm sorry, Ndey Joor. I'm home late again."

"I went to the hospital to see you. I brought you some dinner, even though I know you don't like it when I do that. But I was worried, I didn't know if you had eaten. You weren't there. They told me you left your shift early tonight, with Alioune and Madjigueen, the kind and pretty nurse who watched the kids."

She interrupted herself and looked at her husband tenderly, but Malamine knew that her gaze was also somewhat accusatory, or at the very least filled with worry. Evidently, Ndey Joor knew nothing of his clandestine activities. Out of fear of putting her and the kids in danger, he had naively decided to keep them secret. He hoped that his family would be spared if he was caught. He suddenly grasped the naivety of his reasoning. By getting involved in these activities, he was also involving Ndey Joor, Idrissa, and Rokhaya, whether he liked it or not. Suddenly, keeping this secret seemed absurd to him, especially since Abdel Karim knew his face and his relationship to Ndey Joor Camara.

---

[28] Incense.

"Ndey Joor, I need to tell you . . ."

"I don't want you to tell me what you're doing if you don't want to, Malamine," she interrupted. "I know that if there's something you haven't told me, it's for good reason. Just promise me you'll be careful, and remember that you have children and a wife."

"I want you to know, Ndey Joor. Because what I'm doing may not be wise. But I have to do it. I want you to know, because you're my wife."

He changed, lay down by her side, and cradled her in his arms. The sky began to brighten. The night was beginning to withdraw; some stars grew paler, others were gently cradled by the sun's fiery hue. But in all of its agony, the majestic and noble night still wasn't dead. The day had yet to be born, even though one could sense the proximity of its empire.

He told her everything: the executions he'd witnessed, his decision to act, his meeting with Badji, how he had opened up to others—Ndey Joor knew all of them except Badji—the construction of their secret hideout, their meetings, the acquisition of necessary material, and the creation of the journal. He also told her they had put the final touches on their first issue, which they would distribute the following evening.

Ndey Joor listened calmly without interrupting, her head on her husband's shoulder. When he finished speaking, she said nothing and simply held him close. Malamine couldn't tell if this was a gesture of support or concern. He hid nothing of the risks involved if they were to get caught, and of the threat that this might very well happen.

The first call of the muezzin sounded. Slowly, Kalep awoke.

"Malamine . . . ?"

"Yes?"

"Why are you doing all this?"

She whispered these words but couldn't hide her concern. He held her in his arms to reassure her. A few seconds passed.

"For you, for the kids, for everything we believe in . . ."
Ndey Joor held him tighter.

"And for Ismaïla," he added.

Upon hearing those words, Ndey Joor relaxed and two tears formed at the base of her eyelids. They fell softly and silently down her cheeks, and Malamine felt them wet his chest. He wiped them away and kissed his wife.

PART TWO

I'm happy that I'm able to write to you. They removed my bandages yesterday. I have this strange feeling, as if my arm doesn't really belong to me. As if it's no longer a part of my body.

Since I've come back home, my husband has been avoiding me. He ignores me. I don't know if it's because he's ashamed of what he's done or because he despises me like before. I'm trying to convince myself that he's ashamed, that the reason he hasn't yet apologized is just a question of pride. I hope that deep down his anxiety is eating away at him like acid. That prospect fills me with joy. At night, before falling asleep, I stare at the cold darkness of my room with the same hard look I'd like to give him. I dream that he would kneel at my feet. I dream of seeing him weak, filled with nothing but regret. But none of that happens. I know the truth: he doesn't see me. He has no regrets. There's no weakness on his face. He doesn't look at me. He doesn't speak to me. He doesn't understand me. He doesn't love me. In his eyes, I'm nothing, just an aging woman, incapable of arousing his desire and his love. A useless woman. And so a woman worth beating. A woman to look down upon and objectify. The last time he touched me was to beat me. It's been two years since we've slept in the same bed: I disgust him. But he disgusts me even more. He wanted multiple heirs, but I gave him only Lamine. We tried again, again and again, and again . . . Nothing. Miscarriages. Stillbirths. Then, God's silence. Not even mis-

carriages. Not even stillbirths. Nothing but silence, dryness, barrenness, infertility. I'm a cursed woman. An evil and jealous spirit is keeping me for himself. It's pointless for me to dwell on the life of a barren woman, Aïssata: you know it, everyone knows it. We're human misfortunes. We're the ones who attract tragedy upon our families. We're the ones they beat as a form of exorcism. We're the ones who are unwanted, who are cherished and then abandoned.

I escaped the rejection in the first years because I had my son, Lamine, our eldest. He was proof that I hadn't always been cursed. Proof that I had, at least for one night, been truly desired. Desired. Never loved. Only desired. All these years, how sad . . . How very sad it is to realize that I have perhaps never truly been loved . . .

Except for Lamine . . . He loved me, he protected me as well as he could. As long as he was there, my husband almost never beat me. Ever since our son died, he doesn't hold back, he doesn't think twice. He beats me. He's finally letting go of all the anger and rage that has been building up inside of him for all these years. When he hits me, he shouts, he accuses me of being the cause of Lamine's defiance. It's my fault he's dead, because I failed to instill in him the values of Islam, because I let him follow impious, foreign ways and morals. Because I failed to raise him. We're still the same, Aïssata. A mother is always guilty, as you said. Perhaps that's true, but it's not enough, and we must extend the guilt even further: it's not just all mothers who are guilty, but all women.

Is he right? Did I fail to educate my son? Did I kill him? No. It's those abominable men who killed him. But did I lead him to them? That, I'm not sure. All I ever taught him was love. He loved, and because he loved, they killed him. In this case, love is also to blame. But if love is to blame, then nothing makes sense anymore.

When he beats and blames me, I try to think about all of

this to forget the pain. But I never can. The blows are so violent . . . So I shout, I cry, I scream. I never beg him to stop because it always produces the opposite effect. Only later, when I'm wounded and he has calmed down, do I ask myself this question, the only question one can ask: why is he beating me? Because it's easier to beat a woman than it is to love her.

My husband is a friend of the Brotherhood. He believes that it is destined to rule eternally. All the governments that have killed men failed because they believed they could continue to kill with impunity; all have died from presumption. The Brotherhood can't escape it. This is God's punishment. The stronger they believe themselves to be, the quicker they will fall to the dust.

Have you heard of the underground journal in Kalep? The one condemning the Brotherhood and its crimes? Was it published where you are, too? Since I don't go out, I haven't been able to get my hands on it. One of my neighbors told me about it. Nobody knows where it's from or who wrote it. She just told me that two days ago, in the early morning, the city's people found a stack of copies of a journal called Rambaaj *in every big square and busy area. People found lots of copies in the marketplace, in front of the mosque, in a few of Bantika's famous streets, in the middle of working-class areas. It's practically a divine miracle, it's as if God had done this during the night while everyone was asleep. My neighbor, an old superstitious Muslim woman, believes it's the work of an evil spirit trying to sway the city's people away from their faith. I no longer believe in evil spirits. But I believe in God and his miracles. Miracles that happen because of men alone. If this journal is a miracle, it's a human miracle.*

I don't know what's written in there, I haven't read it, nor do I intend to. I'm not interested, I've had enough. The Brotherhood immediately reacted in Bantika. As soon as they learned of the journal's existence, they increased patrols and searches, they began to conduct investigations, to threaten, to punish. They're looking for people to blame.

The city has become an inferno of fear, and it sits below a cloud of accusation. If that cloud transforms into rain, it will be awful: people will falsely accuse each other for money, for revenge, out of mere suspicion. The city will be grey and dead with fear, and doubt will crush men and destroy their old friendships. We won't love each other anymore. A terrible God will hang over us and watch men kill and betray each other in his name. It will be the end of everything. The journal's name is fitting: it can generate confusion, for better or worse. As always, it'll be up to the people to decide. The Brotherhood or solitude.

Nobody knows what the people will choose. A few weeks ago, they stood behind the Brotherhood. But was this out of conviction or fear? I'm not sure, and I can't know, because everyone's fate is unique. I know that my husband, for example, is Islamist out of conviction, but I also know that my neighbor who spoke to me about all this is Islamist out of fear. They're both members of the people. They are the people. The people exist in them. So, I won't speak about the people, because they are not a single entity. I'd rather speak about men. About each man. The future will depend on what each man chooses to do with his conscience and responsibility. With his freedom. Everything will depend on how each man views his neighbor. If every man gives in to fear, the Brotherhood will win and those who wrote the journal will have done so in vain . . . In order for this journal to make a difference, people can't be scared. But that's asking a lot: fear is our destiny.

Aïssata, I believe a critical period is imminent. I won't be a part of it, I won't be a part of anything. But I hope to witness the return of love. That's the only thing we can hope for, if we can still hope for anything.

Take care of yourself,

Sadobo

PS: In order to avoid anyone finding this letter, I'm having it delivered by my neighbor's daughter. She's taken care of me before. She knows Kalep and will find your house, I trust her. Don't be surprised if the letter is a bit wrinkled or folded: I told her to fold it up and put it in her bra to be safe: if God's pious men decide to search her, one would hope they won't go that far.

CHAPTER 23

bdel Karim was sitting cross-legged on his sheepskin prayer mat: he had a voluminous copy of the noble Quran open beside him. His pipe, which was lit, was clasped in his left palm. If there was one thing that he loved more than going to battle and leading a holy war, it was this moment of complete isolation from the world, which he allowed himself at least once a day, to read the holy Book. Usually, it was after the early afternoon prayer, when the sun is most ruthless, when men go searching for some shade to lie under while digesting their lunch. He retreated to what served as his room in the Islamic Police's quarters. He'd allocate an hour—sometimes two—to prayer, meditation, and the reading of the Quran. He also took advantage of these calm moments to write in his journal, a grimoire of sorts which he'd been updating regularly since joining the Brotherhood. He would document his reflections, insights, adventures, battles, and activities with impeccable regularity. The book had grown to a considerable size over his many years of "service." If we are to believe that even the most savage and ruthless man has, in the depth of his existence, even some brief moments of tenderness, then for Abdel Karim these moments came during the reading of the Quran.

He turned the holy Book's pages gently. With each page, his eyes sparkled, and a tender smile graced his thin lips. For him, this moment of calmness, of reading, of writing, and of secret dialogue with God was a silent jubilation. It was an opportunity to abandon his worries and fears, to become filled with newfound hope, faith, and strength. He read the Quran in a soft voice, whispered the divine verses, caressed the sublime Words that inspired great fascination, fear, and joy in him. The rhythm and effect of these sacred words intoxicated him with delight; he felt the Quran, every verse filled him with an emotion stronger than Love, every word was the sign of God. They trickled through his veins and filled him with a sensation of warmth. He understood everything and, with each reading, this splendid poem inspired by God to save mankind revealed to him new knowledge about the secret of faith and guided him on the path toward Salvation. Abdel Karim had read the Quran a few times, yet was still deeply moved every time he reread it. It was as if, between readings, new meanings formed and flourished among the Book's marvels, as if new revelations trickled straight from them, vibrant and soft like a trail of honey. It was only when he savored this honey that he felt truly happy: he felt close to God and recited the verses to Him. Sometimes the beauty of the words filled his soul, whirling around like celestial music. In times like these, as if overtaken by an unknown and supernatural force, he would raise his voice passionately and recite the verses of the Quran from memory. As his voice amplified, his soul was transported and he felt fulfilled. As Abdel Karim closed his eyes, the words he spoke overwhelmed the room with purity and immersed it in a white light. When these few minutes of ecstasy came to an end and he opened his eyes again, he noticed that he had kneeled without realizing it, his arms spread out, his head thrown back, face toward the sky. He had wept. This had happened a few times already, and he always came out of this trance with vague memories and a face transformed by tender joy.

Outside, the silence was absolute. The Brotherhood had established its quarters in a wealthy neighborhood in the east of Kalep, a stark contrast to the slums of the south. They used an old police office—deserted by the previous occupants—as a command post, a communications center, and administrative offices. A few houses nearby were also empty, as their owners had fled during the first battles, and they used them as their camp. The Brotherhood's men lived and rested here when they were stationed in the city. Finally, the house that once belonged to the former mayor, before he also fled the city, was used as a meeting spot when strategies had to be put into place, information transmitted, and decisions had to be made. This is also where the movement's highest dignitaries stayed when they passed through the city. Abdel Karim was opposed to such a level of comfort, which he believed merely distanced men from their service to God by accustoming them to satanic pleasures of play and idleness. On a number of occasions, he had voiced his concerns to his superior—El Hadj Majidh, the great Muslim judge of the province—about the dangers associated with offering men too many privileges. But his superior always responded that it was nothing to be worried about, that these privileges were God's reward for all they were accomplishing in His Name, and that they were under God's protection. Abdel Karim conceded this and didn't dare object, but he still never held these practices in high regard. He preferred an eremitic way of life, similar to the one he had led during his years of training in the desert. He preferred the harshness of instability to the conveniences of establishment; the former seemed to him more favorable to the cultivation of the soul and the practice of Divine meditation. He was one of those men who found pleasure in life only by living a difficult and modest existence. He believed that by subjecting his body to life's hardships, it would grow strong and resistant while the soul would mature and rise to new heights. He was a man of the desert, a man of the unforgiving sun, a man of sandstorms, a man of burnt faces and arid expanses, a man of frigid and silent nights. He intoxicated himself only with tomorrow's uncertainty, with the fragility of an existence threatened by war and the violence of the elements, hanging only by the thread of God's will.

During the early years, Kalep had offered him all of these things: it was a time when they had to fight against the army of Sumal, which had attempted to take back the city, when they had to defend society in the name of God, when the nights echoed with gunshots, bombshells, and the clamor and cries of men in battle. It was a time when, after finally recapturing the city, they had to bring it back to Salvation, despite the resistance of a population still mired in vice and sin. It was a time when each day presented new dangers, when nerves were tense and life was a perpetual struggle. He didn't dare admit it to himself, but Abdel Karim missed this time. For the past two years, there had no longer been anything authentic to be done in Kalep: the Brotherhood had brought God back, the army had retreated to the southern half of the country. The province was theirs. The road in the desert was theirs. The people had eventually joined their cause. The few summary executions he ordered reminded him briefly of those past jubilations, but they had become too repetitive and commonplace for his liking. Punishing sinners now felt like a mundane part of his routine, and it was a responsibility that he had mostly relinquished to his men. Nowadays, he only attended executions in the capital. Those were the only ones that still gave him the excitement that he was searching for in his duties as chief of the Islamic police. The rare times he felt a rush of adrenaline were when the condemned, whose deaths were imminent, made desperate attempts to cling on to life. He enjoyed looking into their frightened eyes or hearing them utter their final words in delirious agony, a testament to their terrible fear of death. To witness this fear in those who were about to die, to catch their empty gaze, this allowed him to feel the fragility of existence, an existence which nobody can ever truly master. The pleasure he felt in contemplating how death hovers over every man and can, through divine power, crush him in an instant matched the indifference he felt in having men and women executed.

However, over the last few days, a single event had rescued him from his suffocating boredom. Once again, he felt the excitement, the familiar premonition of authentic moments to come. At first, to avoid disappointment, he decided not to get involved in the affair. He entrusted this responsibility to his most trusted men who reported to him daily on the situation's progress.

He was given a copy of the underground publication just a few hours after it came out. He could still picture himself in his tent, writing down a few notes in his journal when one of his lieutenants entered with a document whose pages had been bound by hand. He handed it to him and informed him that his patrol team had found many copies scattered around the city earlier that day. He was also told that some copies had been confiscated, and that more were likely hidden in people's houses and circulating clandestinely. He remembered the raw feeling of joy he felt upon hearing this. But he had left his men in charge of the case because he was convinced that this was a just a small, insignificant uprising which would quickly be dismantled. In the meantime, he read, reread, scrutinized, analyzed, and examined the journal in question.

From his very first reading of the text, he understood that his opponents, while perhaps few in number, were to be feared. They had made the worst possible arguments against the Brotherhood: those taken from the Quran. Each article had been written with a sense of care, calm, and sophistication. Every word was weighed, every argument studied, laid out, proven. It wasn't a text devoid of ideas, like those that generally oppose the Brotherhood all too often are; they were profound, solid ideas, founded on a precise reading of the Quran with examples taken from episodes of the Prophet's life. He was surprised to notice that he even took pleasure from reading certain passages, which he repented immediately with a loud *"Astaghfirullah."* The journal was dangerous, a real threat. If it was circulating among the people it was of the utmost urgency to find those who were hiding it, and even more important to catch the authors, who clearly—as confirmed by the photos of the executions—lived either in Kalep or in the province.

He shuddered. He believed this new and sudden opponent was a challenge orchestrated by God to test his faith, which might have been lacking passion for too long. He had a feeling that the authors of the journal were terrible men, men to be feared, his equals. That very thought made him quiver with delight. That night, he prayed and thanked the Lord for not abandoning him in his pit of boredom.

Despite his wishes, his lieutenants failed to find any information on the journal; of all the houses they searched, they managed to confiscate just a few copies. Abdel Karim stroked his beard. Today, he had decided to take matters into his own hands.

There was also that woman . . .

For the first time in a long time, he felt flustered when he saw her. She seemed so calm, so serene, so strong and soft at the same time . . . Unlike the others, she did not seem to fear or hate him. She had looked at him without apprehension, almost tenderly. He felt bewildered and almost betrayed himself before regaining his composure. Since that day at the hospital, he saw Adjaratou Ndey Joor Camara's face every night before falling asleep; that soft and peaceful face still troubled him. But mainly, he had a feeling that he had seen her before, though he couldn't pinpoint where. This may have been what troubled him the most.

Maybe it was only this. He chased these thoughts out of his

mind and focused on the page of the Quran in front of him. It was the Surah *Al Kaffirun*. He repeated multiple times in a low voice: "*Bismi-l-laahi-r-rahmaani-r-raheem / Qul yaaa ayyouhaal-kaafiroon / Laaa a'budu maa ta'boudoon / Wa laaantum 'aabidoona maaa a'bud / Lakoum deenukum wa liya deen.*"[29]

Then, he stood up and got ready to leave. It was time to find and punish the authors of this journal. He had sworn it on the holy Book.

[29] Surah Al Kaffirun, "The Disbelievers," which says the following:
In the name of God, the All Forgiving, the All Merciful, say, oh unbelievers / I do not adore what you adore / No more than you do not adore what I adore / I never adored what you adore / And you have never adored what I adore / You have your religion and I have mine.

CHAPTER 24

God is gone. He abandoned this world a long time ago, disgusted by its spectacle. Men are alone, they do as they please because everything is permitted. And what they want is Evil: Man is evil, and society makes him even more evil. Sadobo, don't believe that I'm this pessimistic just for the sake of being pessimistic: this is what I see. Hope? Yes, we can allow ourselves to be hopeful, but we need to know what to hope for. I hope for what is certain: sunrise, sunset, the migration of clouds. That's enough for me. Men? What can we expect of them now? What can we expect from men who beat their wives before beating and killing each other? You speak of fear, but fear is not enough. You say fear and I say ignorance. Fear can generate noble emotions and ignite the most grandiose and dignified sentiments in the hearts of men. But this never happens. Fear takes hold of them and does nothing more than bring out their most repressed and animalistic instincts. Their fear of God has led them to fear men, and subsequently to hate them. And because of this, God despairs. And if God himself despairs, why go on? It's useless to try and search for something beyond reality. We must be lucid. But I'm not that desperate, I still have a soul. So, I continue to hope. As I told you: sunrise, sunset, the migration of clouds in the sky. Then sometimes, I add hope. I hope for hope . . .

We never realized how much they loved each other, Sadobo. How both our children loved each other, how much *they believed in what pushed them to the doors of death. I can see them loving each other in the most beautiful way: in hiding. Their love is beautiful because it is threatened. Bold because it breaks the rules. Powerful because it defies danger. Their youth shielded them from fear, their insouciance freed them from the weight of hesitation and consequence. They were foolish. It was wonderful.*

I would give my life to see them love each other again. My little Aïda was beaming before her death . . . To recreate their smiles through memory. Now that's real hope. Imagine them, Sadobo. Just imagine them. The memory of their happiness can appease, even just for an instant, the pain of their loss.

This journal . . . I got my hands on one but only managed to read a few lines. One morning, my husband brought it home. I don't know where he got it, I didn't ask any questions. But he made it clear to me that it had to be read quickly and burned afterwards. I read it. They spoke of our children. An entire article is dedicated to them with a photo of them holding hands and looking at each other right before their death. They were so beautiful and so in love . . . The article was titled "Guilty of Love." I was unable to read all of it. I couldn't even read past the first sentence, which I remember clearly: "They were twenty years old; they died because they loved each other; they were killed in the name of a so-called God of love." I couldn't continue, everything had been said. I threw the journal in the fire and watched it burn. I don't know what to think of it. Like you, I'm scared. Scared that it will produce the opposite effect of what it intended: push people toward indignation. Scared that it will encourage treason. The authors seem to believe in the people's ability to retaliate, to find reasons for fighting back and reclaiming their dignity. They're not just naive, they're guilty. It seems you still believe in each man's ability to rise up and fight for his freedom. I don't believe in that anymore. Men are cowards when their slavery is comfortable. When you shatter that comfort, you destabilize the man and kill the part of him that is a slave. But this journal doesn't shatter any comfort: it goes no further than condemning the horrors. Men don't worry about others in a situation of moral slavery: they worry only about themselves and stay that way so long as their own personal interests remain unscathed. Before my daughter was killed, I had become used to the Brotherhood: I respected its commands and lived comfortably. At that time, no word, phrase, or journal could have pushed me to rebel. Why risk losing my life to an organization that ensures me peace so long as I don't disobey it? It's easy for a man who has no personal worries to obey. It's impossible to make him disobey simply because the overall situation is unbearable. Men are eternally selfish, and they don't get caught up in the general state of the community: they don't worry about the fate of other men and only think about their own comfort, even if that comfort is poisoned.

This journal has made a bet on the people. It will lose because one must never bet on the people: they never do what is expected of them. Sadobo, I allow myself to still call them a people: in the uniformity of their reaction, all of these individuals form a mass that I can call "the people" without being demagogic. I told you: I have no more hope in the people who killed my child. Their reaction when Ndey Joor Camara was beaten? An inexplicable exception to the rule. A coincidence. And the authors of this journal are mistaken if they believe that this reaction was a sign of a potential imminent uprising. This journal has but one goal: to prove to each man that his situation is despicable and that the Brotherhood is poisoning him. It will have to prove that the Brotherhood's God is a barbaric God. Do you believe in that, Sadobo? Do you believe that it's possible, in a single instant, to instill in the soul of a man who has cast stones at another yelling, "Allah Akbar," the idea that the God for whom he has spilt blood is a tyrant? I don't believe so. Those who wrote this journal underestimate how deeply Islamist ideology is rooted in each man. The people that the Brotherhood manipulates through fear are the most dangerous.

Nothing can save these infanticidal people. Nothing, nobody. This land vomits the blood of the innocent. Speaking of God all day is not enough to turn it into a holy land. It's a tainted land.

I don't believe this journal will succeed, Sadobo. Like in Bantika, the Brotherhood has begun to increase its presence and acts of violence. It tracks potential suspects like an animal would its prey. This city, like yours, has become nothing more than posters, threats, wanted notices, and promises of rewards. Kalep has become a fear-ridden hell. But here, the cloud of accusations you mentioned has already transformed into rain. False allegations have begun. Suspicion reigns. It's a race for rewards. Men are ripping each other apart. Their superficial solidarity is crumbling. Where is the Truth in all that? I don't know who the authors of this journal are, but I'd be curious to see their reaction: it was certainly not what they hoped for. What will they do now? They thought they were saving the people: they are tearing them apart. They bet on union, what they got was disunion. They wanted to sprout the seed of revolt, the storm they harvested instead was one of fear and greed.

All of this tires me, Sadobo. I hope I'll be able to go to the cemetery.

Take care of yourself,

Aïssata

I t took them longer than usual, but all seven of them had managed to meet once again. Those who were not from Kalep arrived late due to all the searches they encountered on their journey there. In the basement, Malamine was speaking.

". . . it's true, the situation is no longer in our hands. I believe none of us imagined this outcome. People are reading the journal, but we didn't predict the consequences. People are accusing each other because the Brotherhood promised them rewards for information about our identity. The problem is that they're accusing out of personal vengeance and greed. Those who were caught with copies in their homes, they were beaten. It's not what we wanted and . . ."

"Yes, Malamine," Madjigueen Ngoné interrupted sharply, "but that was fairly clear even before the distribution of the journal. In any case, I was sure of it: a journal, once published, has but one calling: to be read. But what's happening now, especially in Kalep, is something we didn't foresee. We did this work to save people, not to push them toward hating each other, betraying each other, and accusing each other for money. And yet, that's unfortunately what's happening. They're beating people who have copies of the journal in their homes, and other men are accusing and tearing each other apart because of it. I don't think that . . ."

"Calm down, Madjigueen. I am just as disappointed and preoccupied as you are. I completely understand what's happening and what's bothering you. I'm lost, too. It's not what we wanted. I thought these people would be on our side, that the journal would cause a surge."

"Here is the question," said Codou softly, "are we responsible for the people who are being physically punished or wrongly accused because they have copies of the journal in their homes?"

The group became quiet upon hearing these words. Déthié broke the silence:

"Not directly responsible. But I believe we have a moral responsibility toward them, at the very least . . ."

"I was expecting that reaction," said Vieux Faye immediately, "the good old excuse of moral responsibility!"

"Does this idea bother you?"

"When you want to talk about it in relation to the people caught with the journal, yes, it bothers me."

"Please elaborate."

"We are morally responsible only for the journal, for our ideas, for what we have conceptualized and created. But not for anything or anybody else. We've published *Rambaaj* and we stand by it: our responsibility ends there. If you want to extend this morality to those who read it . . ."

"But moral responsibility must extend to these men too, otherwise it doesn't make any sense! Morality has meaning only if it is invoked for the sake of men. To think the way you do is to pretend we live alone, without the others, it's to forget that what we do has consequences. It's totally immoral, Vieux!"

"That's not what I'm saying. We're not alone. But we are free. Each and every man is responsible for what he does. We're responsible for the publication of *Rambaaj*, but we don't force anyone to read it. We left copies in certain areas. From there, the journal took on a life of its own. It's not our responsibility if these people took it, read it, and decided to keep it with them instead of destroying it. Our moral responsibility can't go that far."

"Do you hear yourself? It sickens me that you treat morality with such indifference. We're not only responsible for writing and publishing an underground journal. We are also responsible for its destiny. If every man was responsible only for what he did, the world would disappear, because we would pay attention to nobody else but ourselves. It would be the end of morality, of man, of love, of everything. We're not machines!"

"Stop throwing slogans around, Déthié. I'm talking to you about a concrete situation, not noble ideas."

"I'm also talking to you about a specific situation relating to people, not ideas."

"In that case, do you really believe that we are to blame if people choose to read the journal and get caught? *Rambaaj* is intended to bear witness and to condemn. It wasn't published in a random time or place, it was published during a time of crisis, of barbarism. This isn't the time to wallow in self-pity. If we have to stop and think every time our journal causes a backlash for the sake of moral responsibility, we might as well admit to ourselves that we're not going to get anywhere, that the journal is a failure, betrayed by the very people who published it. What a sad fate!"

"I'm with you, I refuse to ignore individual lives for the sake of the superb and irrepressible unfolding of History."

"Are you really the one saying this?" Vieux Faye answered with a chuckle. "You who, just a few days ago, were still triumphantly claiming that 'the brutalities of progress are called revolutions'? You who accepted that men might be mistreated so long as they are walking toward their freedom? You who legitimized violence if it encouraged the progress of the human race? Wasn't that all you, Déthié?"

"There's a difference between legitimizing violence when it's necessary, by accepting it and learning the moral lessons it teaches us, and legitimizing violence by thinking of it as a simple fact of nature, an inevitable law, and not as something created by responsible men. Any revolution not carried out in the name of morality—in other words, in the name of men—loses its spirit and its truth. We can't ignore that fact."

"Calm down, please," begged Malamine. "The problem is so serious that we shouldn't aggravate it by letting it tear us apart. We understand both your positions well. I suggest that we go around the table to figure out what we should do. Would you start, Père Badji?"

"This journal no longer belongs to us. It has taken on a life of its own. That's all I have to say," answered Père Badji.

"I think," continued Madjigueen, "that others shouldn't have to pay the price for what we created. Yes, they decided to keep the journal, but we're the ones who offered it to them. They didn't ask for it. From the moment we lent out our hand, we enlisted them to join our cause, and we became responsible for them. So yes: we do have a moral responsibility toward them. I suggest we refrain from printing and limit ourselves to what's been done. Sure, we can't do much now, but we can at least prevent other people from getting caught and being tortured."

"But what you fail to understand, or at least pretend not to understand," yelled Vieux Faye, whose voice was now trembling with frustration, "is that even if we put an end to this, people are still going to be stopped, tortured, beaten, and killed. Whether we like it or not. Whether we fight or not. I thought you understood this! Our moral responsibility, or lack thereof, changes nothing. To use your expression, this journal enlisted all those who read it. There's no going back. If we really want something to change, we're going to have to go through with it until we either succeed or fail brilliantly, despite the dead and the tortured."

"I tend to agree with Vieux Faye," said Alioune calmly. "We must continue. Madjigueen, I think we shouldn't underestimate the strength of those who kept the journal with them and were caught. I'm inclined to believe it's a sign that we touched on something essential. And if we have any sort of moral responsibility toward them, it's to continue to fight and distribute the journal. For the sake of hope."

"Your wisdom will always surprise me, Alioune. I agree with your arguments," said Codou, smiling. "We must continue. We have a responsibility to them: we can't abandon them now."

"What do you think, Malamine?" asked Déthié abruptly, clearly still agitated after his exchange with Vieux Faye.

"I think that in times like these, there are no guarantees. And the only way not to get discouraged is to maintain a sense of direction despite the uncertainty. We can't forget that there is a superior dimension that commands all action: consciousness. We must always act without losing sight of the fact that we must be human. We must fight humanely, with human means, that's the issue."

"What does that mean, in simpler terms?" asked Codou smiling.

"I mean that despite everything, we must continue to fight. Shutting our eyes to the horrors won't stop them from proliferating. We'll print again tonight, if you agree. Déthié?"

"I was never against the idea of continuing. I simply wanted to draw attention to the fact that we can't forget that there are other men who we must take into account in every decision that we make. I vote to continue."

"Very well. And you, Madjigueen?"

"I would prefer that we stop, at least for a time. Perhaps you overestimate the strength and determination of these people. They found a journal, naturally they took it to read it and got caught. If I continue, I feel that I'm betraying the very cause I signed up for. I signed up to fight for men. I cannot accept the thought that it's because of me that these men are now suffering. They didn't ask me for anything. I will stop. I won't be part of the next publication. I'm sorry. I taught Vieux Faye how to create the electronic template for the journal. He will be able to do it from now on. That's what I had to say."

"I think everyone understands and respects your decision. We will miss you. On behalf of everybody here, thank you for what you've done."

Madjigueen started to tear up as her six—now former—partners applauded her. Déthié spoke again.

"Nonetheless, I think that we should wait a while before distributing the paper. We won't get very far with all the inspections and searches. Let's wait for them to fall asleep again and then . . ."

At that very moment, they heard a faint noise. Although the bar was closed and it was nighttime, someone seemed to be knocking on the door. A heavy silence settled in, encouraging them all to listen attentively, to wait and see if the noise persisted. It did. They were long, steady, determined knocks. They were strong enough to be heard from the basement, which was located below the closed restrooms at the back of the bar's main room on the opposite end from the front door. They all listened, hoping that the noise would finally come to a stop. Every one of them hoped it was a lost person, a drunk, or even a homeless man, but nobody wanted or even dared to think that it could be the patrol. Nobody had heard the sound of a car or sirens. That could be a good sign, but also a bad one. And what if they were caught, tricked?

They got scared.

"Nobody make a sound," whispered Malamine. "I'll go. Stay here and don't move. If it's the militia, I'll figure out how to drive them away. I'm going to lock you in when I leave; you'll have to turn the lights off in case there's a search. In any case, we have to stay calm, no matter what happens."

"It wouldn't make any sense for you to be here at this time.

I'll go. I'm the owner of the bar and the one they're expecting to see. Don't move, don't even breathe. And," Père Badji said in a tone that required no reply, "no matter what happens, don't try and get out of here until I reopen the hatch. I will do so only if the coast is clear."

Before anybody could say a word, Père Badji went upstairs and closed the hatch on his friends. They could hear the characteristic sound of his cane on the tiles. Then, there was complete silence, with the exception of the persistent knocking, relentless like a trumpet on Judgment Day. They waited, each of them praying silently.

CHAPTER 26

Père Badji walked slowly toward the door, which was still being pounded on at regular intervals. As usual, his face was serene, indifferent, immune from fear. His pipe stuck firmly between his lips as he crossed over to the other side of the bar where the lights were still on. He arrived at the door.

He opened it. Through the half-opened door appeared the silhouette of a man whose right hand was clenched into a fist and strangely suspended at chest level: he was getting ready to knock again and had been interrupted by the door's sudden opening. At first, the old man had a hard time recognizing the features of his late-night guest. It was dark and the few street-lights scattered about the neighborhood weren't functioning properly, switching on and off erratically, so outdated that they made an electric crackling sound. Père Badji squinted his eyes; his visitor, on the other hand, remained still. They stayed like this for some time, without a word, as if each man was surprised to see the other. The two masters of silence were facing one another, ready to push each other to the very boundaries of mutism. Each was gauging his power through the other's gaze, attitude, and body language. Both men, though experts in self-control, clashed silently and violently. One of them had to surrender for the battle not to go on all night.

"*Assalam Aleïkum.* I am Captain Abdel Karim Konaté, chief of Kalep's Islamic Police."

"I am Badji, owner of this establishment."

Each of them was brief and concise. While the confrontation started in silence, it continued through speech. Hearing this first exchange was like hearing a reenactment of this legendary dialogue: "I am Alexander the Great." "And I Diogenes the Cynic."

"May I enter?"

"What do you want?"

"I just told you: to enter."

"Why do you want to enter?"

"To speak with you."

Père Badji moved to the side. He didn't want his zealousness to stir up any suspicion. Père Badji was able to guess from his attire, his extraordinary restraint, and the majestic control with which he lowered his hand, that Abdel Karim was one of those men who feared nothing. His impeccable flair made him seem almost invincible. He had a certain aura about him, something frightening. The old man took a puff from his pipe. If he had been alone he wouldn't have allowed such a man to enter his place. But he was not alone, and he remembered that below them were his friends, and that the man in front of him was probably searching for them. Badji decided to face his opponent diplomatically.

The captain entered, and the old man was finally able to examine his stature and expression. He was immediately struck by his face, which was part man, part beast.

Abdel Karim walked slowly toward the bar and stopped. The old man didn't move and remained near the door. The captain turned his back to him.

"So then, you are the owner of this bar, the famous Père Badji."

Badji didn't answer and continued to stare at Abdel Karim, who had now turned around to face him.

"I've heard many things about this place from my men," he continued.

"Indeed, I've never had the honor of seeing you here. At least not until tonight."

"I'm afraid that will never happen, Aladji Badji. You know what Islam says about places like these."

"I don't sell anything illegal, Captain. You can check if you'd like. And your men, who visit quite frequently, can attest to it."

"My men . . . surely they could, if I asked them. But even if you served them alcohol and salted pork, they wouldn't say a word. I'm well aware that some of them have questionable morals. Even those in God's service can't escape vice."

He interrupted himself and slowly embraced the room with his gaze, as if looking for a specific object.

"That's your rifle, up there?"

"Yes."

"Very nice model."

"Thank you, Captain."

Abdel Karim looked at it for some time, then continued:

"Believe me, Père Badji, when the time comes, I will personally take care of those who are sullying God's name. I will deal with those who are working secretly, in the shadows, to bring the Devil back to this city."

"I don't doubt that for a second, Captain," said Père Badji as calmly as he could.

They looked at each other in silence for a few seconds. Abdel Karim smiled.

"Surely you must be asking yourself why I'm paying you a visit this late."

"Indeed, I'd like to know."

"I'm getting there, Aladji. Thank you for letting me in."

"You didn't leave me a choice," answered the old man.

"That's true. But I wouldn't have allowed myself to insist if I was not confident that you were still awake. I saw the lights of the bar were still on despite the hour. I thought to myself that maybe . . ."

"I was going over my expenses, as you can see next to you," interrupted the old man while pointing to an open notebook with his cane. He had been cautious to place it there, on a table.

"Oh, but, Aladji, you do what you want, you are in your own place, and I will never judge you for not going to sleep: I myself know all too well the torment of insomnia. But . . ."

"But what?"

Père Badji immediately regretted this abrupt response which might have given away his frustration or uneasiness. Thankfully, the man facing him failed to notice, or at the very least pretended not to.

"Well, while I was patrolling the neighborhood, I believe I heard a lively discussion unraveling, one which seemed to have originated from your bar. Where could it have come from at such a late hour? At first, I thought maybe it was my men who were here arguing. But then I saw the bar was closed. And now I see it's empty. You have to admit it's rather strange."

"Indeed."

"Ah! So . . ."

"So, as you can see, it's just us two, Captain."

"And upstairs?"

"I live alone, ever since you burned my dog, Captain Konaté. Am I not allowed?"

"Oh yes, yes, Aladji. Please excuse what might come off as an inappropriate breach of privacy. And be thankful to the Brotherhood for distancing you from those diabolical animals. While I may be disturbing you," he said without seeming worried about Badji's scornful pout, "it's not to delve into your private life. I was intrigued by these animated voices in the dead of night. Who wouldn't have been? I'm certain I heard them, and almost certain they came from your bar. It's strange."

"It sure is."

"What do you make of it?"

"That you are human."

"God attests to that. I am his creation. So?"

"So, like every human being, you can be mistaken."

"I am never mistaken."

This frightening reply was spoken with such truth and conviction that at no point did Père Badji believe it was purely rhetorical. The man facing him was, indeed, a man who was never mistaken.

"I'm happy to believe you, Captain. But God can sometimes play with our senses, no?"

"God can do anything."

"So, let's say that this is what must have happened tonight."

"Why would he have done this?"

"Are the ways of the Lord not impenetrable?"

"God is Mystery."

"So?"

"What you say is possible, surely. Maybe we simply had to meet."

"I can't think of any other reason. You can see with your own eyes that there is no one here. You can check, if you'd like."

"That won't be necessary."

"Good, that would have inconvenienced me. And see? You can't even hear any voices."

"They are quiet now. God must have quieted them," responded Abdel Karim with an enigmatic smile.

"Well then, if your concerns were just about this, rest assured," said the old man. He made vague gestures as he was talking, the kind a host makes to signal to his guest that he has overstayed his welcome and it's time to leave.

"Of course, Père Badji. But . . ."

"Yes, Captain?"

"May I know why you are closed earlier than usual tonight?"

"I told you: I was going over the books."

"Ah! You close every time you go over your books?"

"I have no other way. I manage this place alone."

"You must go over them quite a fair amount, then. For the last two years, I have often overheard my men complaining, on their way back from patrolling, that they weren't able to come in for some hot tea."

"I often go over my books. And I have to close the bar when I do so."

"Indeed, I've noticed."

"What do you mean?'

"Sometimes, during my walks, I happen to pass by your closed bar. I think I can also confidently say that you usually go over your books on Thursdays."

"That's right."

"And that there was a time when you would go over them every Thursday."

"That's correct."

"And other times you did not go over them for a while."

"Business must not have been so good."

"And you went over them just a few days ago."

"I did."

"And you are going over them again today!"

"There can't be any errors."

"Looking for errors the other day was not enough?"

"It's important to fight off boredom."

"Always!"

"Every day, if my age permitted."

"What a remarkable work ethic you have!"

"Business cannot survive with laziness and approximation."

"I agree."

"So, it's settled."

"I admire you."

"I don't deserve it."

"If I were not Abdel Karim, I would like to be like you."

"I take that as a compliment, one that honors me and speaks highly of you."

"One more thing, please . . . Whose scooter is that, the one parked outside in front of the bar? I have to admit I can't really imagine you on that contraption."

Père Badji was shaking, but managed to maintain a perfectly detached and indifferent demeanor. Vieux Faye, who usually came via bus, had mentioned his "new scooter" earlier, which Père Badji had completely forgotten about. As someone who was always so cautious, he blamed himself for letting this minor detail slip his mind, especially because it could easily give them away.

These thoughts raced through his mind within a fraction of a second.

"Someone left it with me."

"Who?"

"A friend."

"So, you have friends?"

"Who doesn't?"

"Misanthropes. I was told you are one of them."

"You were either lied to or misinformed."

Abdel Karim smiled once more. Badji remained stoic and maintained eye contact while clenching his pipe. The silence in the room was almost unsettling.

"If you don't mind, Captain, I'd like to go to sleep," said Badji after some time. "I'm exhausted after crunching all these numbers."

"Of course, Aladji. But before I go, if you will allow it, I'd like to speak with you briefly about a topic that is dear to my heart."

"Ah! What is it?" said Père Badji, pretending to be surprised.

"Do you believe in the Brotherhood?"

"I believe in God."

"In that case, you are a trustworthy man. Here's my problem: a few days ago, you must've heard about a journal bashing the Brotherhood's practices . . ."

In that instant, Abdel Karim paused and scrupulously examined the old man's face, trying to get something out of him. The old man was trying as hard as he could to maintain eye contact with the Demon and, in a moment of absentmindedness, dropped his cane.

"I must have heard about it from someone, yes."

"Did you read it?"

"I don't know how to read."

"And write?"

"No."

"How do you go over your expenses?"

"In Arabic. I can't read or write in French."

Père Badji surprised himself with the spontaneity of his reply. Clearly a man's perils are the measure of his courage.

"And what do you think of this journal?"

"I told you: I haven't read it."

"Yes, but you must think something of it."

"Nothing that is very original or worthy of developing."

"That interests me."

"Why?"

"I hold you in high regard."

"Well, if you insist, I think that in everything there is some element of truth. There must be an element of truth in this journal, but I could not tell you what it is."

Abdel Karim stood up and walked toward the exit. As he reached the old man, whose stature was insignificant compared to his own, he stopped and looked at him for a long while. Père Badji took on this challenge for the umpteenth time.

"You are a unique man, Père Badji. You are well respected

in this city. People admire you. I need people like you. To set the example."

"I'm my own person, Captain."

"It wasn't an offer."

"What was it?"

"Nothing worth developing for the time being," he responded, smiling.

He opened the door and turned around once more to face the old man. His face no longer bore a smile. There was something cold and ruthless about him. This reminded Père Badji that the man standing in front of him wasn't exactly a man at all: he was both more than that and less than that.

"Aladji Badji, know that I swore to catch the authors of this journal and all of those who might have helped them. I'll catch them with my own hands."

"I hope you do, but why are you telling me this, Captain?"

"I don't know, Père Badji. But perhaps you, you do know," he added after a brief silence. "*Assalamu aleïkum.*"

The old man had not yet responded when Abdel Karim closed the door behind him and faded into the night.

Père Badji fell on the first chair he found. He hadn't noticed but he was sweating lightly, even though the night was unexpectedly cool.

CHAPTER 27

A fraid that Abdel Karim might spot them, they had no other choice but to wait until daylight to leave the bar. The chief's visit, the things he had alluded to and insinuated—it was unclear if they were ironic or serious—and, most importantly, his enigmatic last words had left them terribly worried. They went their separate ways after deciding to let a few days pass before attempting to distribute the journal on a large scale again. This gave them some time to reflect on the situation and see how it would evolve.

Before leaving, Madjigueen Ngoné said her goodbyes to everyone, especially to those who didn't live in Kalep and whom she may not have the opportunity to see again. In spite of his poorly disguised contempt and distant behavior, Vieux Faye seemed particularly affected by the young woman's departure. They had grown closer over the course of their meetings, despite their natures and temperaments which were so conflicting that it seemed impossible for them to get along. What they had couldn't exactly be referred to as a relationship; it was the kind of interaction that wavers somewhere between friendship, tenderness, compassion, complicity, mutual irritation, and perhaps even love. Nobody really knew what was going on between the two of them. Did they even know? They were all surprised—Madjigueen Ngoné and Vieux Faye especially—when Vieux Faye interrupted the young woman during their debate. It was less about the fact that they disagreed—because this happened often—and more about the way that they had expressed this disagreement. Usually, even when it came to serious matters, their discussions were always light-hearted. Although their conflicting opinions pushed them further apart, in the end the way they articulated this conflict would always bring them closer together. This is how their bond flourished, as a bond often does: through mockery, tender opposition, and playful teasing. But today, for unknown reasons, Vieux Faye was particularly grim and aggressive, even with his lovely friend. And it would've been useless to try and understand exactly why. Maybe it was because of his bitter interaction with Déthié moments earlier. Or maybe because of his stubbornness. Perhaps he was just in a bad mood.

Still, when the time came to bid each other farewell, Vieux Faye suddenly felt bad about the situation and his behavior, which saddened him even further. Madjigueen was the last one to say goodbye. They hoped their embrace would be short, but it was unexpectedly long. The others, who had understood that they were sharing in something greater than just their immediate sadness, had moved away to give them some privacy. No one knows what words they exchanged. They simply noticed that once they joined them again, the tears that Madjigueen had tried so hard to hold in were streaming down her cheeks. And that Vieux Faye seemed stunned.

Then they left one after the other, according to the usual procedure. Vieux Faye didn't turn back to look at Madjigueen when he left.

She left after him, making sure to look away from where his scooter was parked. She hurried off to fade into the crowds of Kalep, both to get lost and to seek refuge. It was as if she feared that Vieux Faye was still there trying to find her. But he was gone, and nobody was trying to find her. She walked, letting fate guide her, passing by thousands of faces without bothering to look at them.

CHAPTER 28

I t's hot and Madjigueen Ngoné is walking through the city. She doesn't know what to think about herself: she doesn't believe she's a coward, yet that's how she feels after making the decision to leave her friends. But on the other hand . . . All these faces whom she had implicitly committed to fight for through the journal hadn't asked for anything: these were the faces of independent people who acted according to their own will. They could not be taken hostage under any circumstance, nor could one make any assumptions about their wishes, desires, or courage. But, she asked herself, what exactly does courage look like right here and now in Kalep? What does that word mean to the woman she just crossed in the street? Or to that child playing? She watches the people of Kalep. They go about their business, battle their own demons, fight their own fears, and come to terms with death. This can take on different forms: some collaborate, others keep quiet, and some rebel. Ultimately, they all survive. In her eyes, surviving is the most difficult thing a person can do. It's harder than courage, harder than rebellion, perhaps even harder than love. Survival transcends these things because it's in the name of survival that people often demonstrate courage, rebellion, and love: survival of our families, of ourselves, of what we believe in, of those we cherish, of a happy world that we've grown to know and love. But survival above all else. And according to Madjigueen Ngoné, that's what these people are doing: surviving, clinging on to life as best they can in a world of death.

Madjigueen Ngoné feels a sense of relief. She tells herself

she was right to leave her friends: their cause may be very noble, but they pretend to know those they are trying to help. But these people can never truly be known. No one can pretend to know the internal battles and drives that move them, that inspire them to get up in the morning, and that motivate them to survive. What her friends failed to understand is that the people's priority is survival. We can't ask them to rebel, because their instinct for survival is already stronger than even the great-est resistance. But what is survival without dignity and honor? It's a matter of principle, of morality. Madjigueen doesn't linger on that thought. Those who have the luxury of choosing their means of survival do not truly know survival, the kind that doesn't allow for the leisure of preference, the kind that can be summed up in the following dilemma: "survive or die." When we must survive, truly survive, when we have no other choice but to survive, what is the meaning of courage? What does it mean to be brave in front of a firing squad?

She now has the answer to all of these questions: the only true form of courage is survival, it's fighting against the death drive, it's refusing to give in to the desperation that causes sui-cide, to the selfishness that leads to betrayal. Trying to survive for ourselves and for those we love. Doing everything we can to keep them alive. Surviving not for great ideas, but for the simple primal idea of survival upon which all other ideas are built. Surviving in order not to die. Nothing more. Nothing less. In the most honorable way possible. As she walks toward the square, she realizes that she's thinking about dignity again. Her answer is a compromise. But is man himself not a com-promise? Madjigueen doesn't want to engage with this new idea. She smiles as these thoughts enter her mind and float away. She knows that they are perhaps futile. Nobody takes the time to notice the worry and tension on her face, because everyone is too busy surviving.

She continues walking through the city.

CHAPTER 29

O ut of caution, Ndey Joor Camara still tried not to lean her back against any surfaces. She no longer wore a bra because of the heat, and dressed only in light camisoles. Her wounds were beginning to scab, but she was still in pain. She heard someone enter the room she was resting in.

"Is that you, sweetie?" she said without looking toward the door.

"Oh, how did you know it was me? I wanted you to guess."

"Yeah? And how would you have made me guess? I would've recognized your voice immediately."

Ndey Joor Camara turned around and smiled at Rokhaya.

"Well ... I would've used Dad's voice, then Idrissa's. That's how!"

She entertained Ndey Joor by imitating both men of the house. Then, satisfied with her performance, the child got into the bed next to Ndey Joor, who was now sitting, and laid her head on her mother's knees. Ndey Joor stroked her hair tenderly as she whispered a song.

Rokhaya had grown. She had grown because now she had a general idea of what was going on: men were dying, dogs were being burnt alive, her mother had been beaten. She understood all of this. Innocence was no longer possible, nor was living out one's childhood: but that's war.

Ndey Joor noticed her daughter had grown up since she had protected her the day her back was torn to pieces. Without realizing it, the young girl almost never played anymore.

"Are you still in pain, Mom? Do your wounds still itch?"

Ndey Joor Camara stopped singing but continued to caress her daughter's head. Rokhaya's eyes were closed and she'd spoken to her mother without moving, in a voice filled with disarming innocence.

"No, darling, it doesn't hurt anymore."

"Really?"

"Yes, really, sweetie. You took great care of me: you, your brother, and your father. That's why it doesn't hurt anymore. Because you're here. Every time I feel like it hurts, I think about you and it calms me. Do you understand?"

"Yes, Mom, I understand. I think I understand. Mom . . ."

The young girl turned her head toward her mother and opened her eyes. When she noticed them, Ndey Joor couldn't help but think of her own mother's eyes. That was one of the many traits—her name being one of them—that Rokhaya had inherited from her.

"Yes, darling?"

"I'm sorry you were hurt. It's because of me. I'm sorry and I never thanked you. Forgive me, I disobeyed you that day. You yelled at me to stay inside the house, but I still came out to join you. I couldn't stay in the house. I wanted to be with you."

Ndey Joor Camara's heart tightened at the sight of this little face overcome by such painful thoughts. Rokhaya was still looking at her, sad but wary, as if hoping for an answer, an excuse, a comforting word, maybe even a scolding. Ndey Joor could read terrible desperation in her eyes, a stark contrast to the innocence of her youthful face. She stayed like this for a while, unable to respond. She continued to stroke her daughter's hair with what is arguably the essence of motherhood: immeasurable tenderness.

"You're the one who saved my life that day, Rokhy," she finally managed to tell her daughter.

"Me? But how, Mom? Don't you remember? You're the one who protected me and covered me with . . ."

"Yes, I remember very well, sweetie. I remember it as if it were yesterday. I remember everything that happened that day."

"So why do you say that I saved you? I couldn't have, Mom, I was in your arms and you were holding me so tight that I couldn't move. How could I have saved you?"

"If you hadn't been there, I would have cried out. That's how you saved me. It was very brave of you, darling. I should be the one to thank you."

"Really?"

"Really."

Rokhaya smiled, relieved. She closed her eyes once more. Ndey Joor Camara was about to sing again when Rokhaya stopped her.

"You know, Mom, that day, I . . ."

She paused for a few seconds.

"What happened that day, darling? Why did you stop talking?"

"Because what I'm about to say is impossible, you're going to think it's another one of my inventions."

"Tell me anyway, and I'll also tell you an impossible story. You'll see, we all have a story that only we believe in. What happened that day?"

"You promise you won't tell Idrissa? He'll make fun of me and tell me I'm a child who still wears diapers and believes in fairy tales."

"He also used to believe in fairy tales. But if it makes you happy, I won't say a word to him, or to your father. It'll stay between us. Tell me."

"Well, that day, while I was in your arms I was crying, remember?"

"Yes, darling, I remember."

"It wasn't because I was scared, you know. It wasn't even because I had a small cut on my hand."

Ndey Joor Camara looked at her, curious.

"It's because I could feel it every time they beat you. It's as if the whip went through your body and touched mine. I know it's not possible and it must be my imagination, but that's it. Every time that man hit you, I screamed louder because I felt it. You were silent, and I was screaming for you. Do you understand? There. That's what I wanted to tell you. Don't forget you promised not to tell Idrissa!"

"No, I won't tell him a thing, sweetie. He wouldn't understand."

"Yeah, I know. But you, do you understand?"

"I think so, darling. I understand. Thank you for screaming for me. That's how I would have liked to scream."

"Then why didn't you?"

"Because then the man hitting me would have thought that he was hurting me."

"He wasn't hurting you?"

"Yes, of course he was, but I didn't want to show him. That's why I didn't shout. And also because you were there, and you shouted for me."

"Oh, so you knew it too?"

"Yes."

The little girl smiled, satisfied by the deep bond that had just formed between her and her mother.

Ndey Joor began to sing softly again. She sang an old song that her mother had taught her when she was only a bit older than Rokhaya. It was a hymn that the women from her village sang together in the fields to keep their courage and spirits up. Under the sun with their sickles, baskets, elastics, and knives, their loins girded and their faces covered in sweat, they sang. Standing one behind the other, they formed long lines with each woman in charge of a particular task. They continually

vied to be the most passionate in their song, and with each chorus the tune was imbued with new breath and vitality. Each
row of women sang, echoing the chorus of the ones before, as
if trying to outshine them in both the beauty of their melody
and the rigor of their rendering. Meanwhile, the song was per-
petually subject to embellishment, additions, and lyrical
improvisations, which distracted the workers' minds and
immersed them in the abundance of their effort and the difficulty of their task. The women were so absorbed by the rhythm
and variations of this song that they forgot about the brutal
sun, which no longer burned the backs of their necks as badly.
They walked together at a steady pace and to the beat of the
rhythm, slowly advancing on the vast expanses that retreated
toward the horizon. Ndey Joor Camara still remembered the
first time she grabbed a spot in one of the rows alongside her
mother. She'd been a strong, imposing woman whose powerful and striking voice outshone the others'. She was always in
the first row, front and center. She was the one to begin the
song and set the pace, speeding up if necessary and slowing
down when the women were walking too fast. She would
decide when to pause and when to stop. Ndey Joor remembered the overwhelming sense of exhaustion that overcame her
after a long day's work. But mostly, she remembered the
euphoria, the overwhelming feeling of warm and tender joy as
her mother, a few feet away, watched her with warring expressions of love and pride.

Every time she felt nostalgic about these times, she'd hum
one of the songs that the women would sing during their long
days of work. When she closed her eyes, she could still see the
vast horizons.

"Tell me, Mom . . ."

"Yes, my child?"

"Do you think that one day everything will go back to how
it was before? That the people with the turbans and guns will

leave? That I'll be able to go outside and play again without being scared? Do you think that the dogs will return, and that people will be able to organize parties outside?"

"I don't know, Rokhy. But I hope so. I pray for it every day."

"It's funny, Mom: you're the first person not to respond 'yes' when I ask that question. It's as if everyone else felt they had to respond 'yes.' Not because they really believe it, but because they're trying to comfort me, or maybe to comfort themselves. I don't know. But that's also normal, don't you think?"

"What is?"

"That everyone is trying to comfort themselves by telling themselves that these people will leave soon."

"Some of them really do believe it, sweetie. Do you believe it?"

"I don't know, Mom. I'm too little for all these things. Dad told me he believed it, and that he was certain that they'd leave soon. But he never said how they'd leave. I also asked Idrissa last night."

"Oh yes? And what did he say?"

"First he said the same thing you did, that he didn't know. Then, after a few moments, he said that he didn't believe it, and that the people in turbans would stay in Kalep for a long time. I wanted to ask him why he thinks that, but he went up to his room. I'd like to ask him."

"We can ask him together later, if you'd like."

"Yes, Mom, I'd like that. We'll ask him together when he's done talking to Dad. He's the one who told me to leave them alone because they had to talk. That's why I came to see you. I want to know what they're talking about for once . . ."

"For once?"

"Didn't you notice that they don't talk to each other much? I noticed that. It's as if they won't dare speak to each other or even look at each other for too long. Do you know what they could be talking about? It's a boys' thing, isn't it?"

"That's it . . . a boys' thing. We'll also have our little meeting between us girls too, and we won't tell the boys anything. We'll have our own little secrets. I think we already have a few."

"Ah! You promised me you'd teach me how to make *curray*! Now's the time!"

Ndey Joor Camara, amused, stood and went to the corner of the room to get a silver incense burner. But all she could focus on was her husband and her son.

CHAPTER 30

H ow did he react?" asked Ndey Joor Camara.
"As expected, or almost: he showed no emotion.
Even though I thought, only thought, I may have
seen a spark of surprise in his eyes. Nothing I do seems to
affect him, not even that. He didn't seem happy, disappointed,
or angry. God knows I would've preferred that to his complete
lack of a response."

Ndey Joor Camara grabbed her husband's hand and placed
her lips softly against it before pressing it gently to her cheek.
It was futile for her to speak. Her husband simply needed her
to be by his side.

She suffered greatly from the distance between Malamine
and her son. She witnessed the silent family drama unfolding
before her eyes and couldn't do anything about it. She was the
first to notice that her husband and son were becoming increasingly distant, even though they wouldn't admit it to themselves.
She was the first to notice that an unbridgeable gap was fatally
growing between them. She tried to act as soon as she understood this wasn't an illusion, which was right around the time
that Malamine was starting to become less present for reasons
she would only be made aware of later on. Only then did she
decide to try and salvage this inevitably crumbling connection.
But by that point, it was already too late. Seldom at home,
Malamine kept postponing the conversation that his wife had
asked him, on numerous occasions, to have with Idrissa.
Idrissa, on the other hand, would systematically deny the

distance between him and his father, with too much composure and calmness for it to have been true. To justify why he
didn't speak much, he'd add that he was an introvert of solitary nature. This was true, and Ndey Joor knew that he was not
very communicative: but he hadn't always been that way.
Idrissa had gone mute at the very time that Ndey Joor realized
he was distancing himself from his father.

The drama continued. The distance grew so deep that it
was difficult to imagine a time when it didn't exist. Idrissa was
quiet. Malamine worked. Ndey Joor suffered. She was mother
of the former, wife of the latter, friend of the two, and she knew
that the biggest mistake she could make was to take sides. She
didn't want to blame one or the other; she wanted to continue
loving them both equally and refused to think of one of them
as guilty. She didn't always succeed, though. She would blame
herself whenever her protective motherly instinct overrode her
commitment to her husband, or the other way around. This
implicit separation between the two men in her life persisted,
all the while she was fighting her own battle: the fight to
remain a woman. Not a wife, not a mother, not a confidante,
not a friend, but wife, mother, confidante, and friend all at
once. Sometimes at her son's bedside, other times in her husband's arms, always in between the two, she clung to their
imaginary sleeves, trying to keep them from drifting further
apart, inviting them to join her in an embrace. Even though she
sometimes failed, she refused to surrender or give in to her
desperation in the same way that she dismissed false hope. She
wouldn't comment when Malamine mentioned that Idrissa
seemed unmoved by what he said. She simply held him close,
taking advantage of the soothing heat of his hand on her cheek.

"Maybe I'm just a bad father, Ndey Joor."

"I forbid you from saying that, Malamine. When are you
going to stop feeling responsible for everything that's happening?"

She spoke without anger, but rather with a softness which strengthened her argument. And she was right. Malamine immediately regretted the words he spoke.

"I'm sorry. I'll talk to him tomorrow. I'll try again. I'm his father, and it's my job to approach him. Maybe I'm not an excellent father, but I have the right and the obligation to be close to my son: we've grown apart. I haven't really known my son in a very long time."

"He's grown up, Malamine. And so many things happened in between. This nasty war, this nasty regime, the siege of Kalep: all of it weighs on the heart, and men are forever changed by it. We don't even realize how much these events are silently affecting us. Idrissa is now all grown up, and he was barely a teenager when this all started. Today, he's a man, and he has been for a long time. I told you, he grew up faster than anyone. Look at him, when he eats or walks, or when he reads, or even when he's just lost in thought. That shadow, that silence, that concentration, the sad seriousness on his face: they all belong to a mature man who doesn't know what's happening to him. Simply because no one explained to him that he was growing up. Nobody taught him how to become a man in such a short time. He was forced to do it alone, with what was left of his childhood, with all of his mistakes, regrets, fears, gaps in knowledge, and pain. I think . . . I think he just needs somebody to tell him that being a man doesn't necessarily mean giving up the kingdom of childhood."

Malamine didn't respond. Once again, Ndey Joor had conveyed truths which he had been completely ignorant of up until that point. Or at the very least, these were truths that had not yet led to painful and confusing realizations. He thought back to that time when he would wander through Kalep, unable to remember exactly when that was. Idrissa would jump around happily by his side, asking him a thousand and one questions that he sometimes didn't know how to answer. It seemed as though that time had never existed.

Malamine tilted his head and leaned it against his wife's. For the first time in many long months, he wasn't thinking of the journal, of his friends, of the Brotherhood, or of Abdel Karim. He was thinking about his family, specifically about Idrissa. But more than anything, he felt profoundly sad and alone, even though his wife was by his side.

CHAPTER 31

They were just about to have dinner when there was a knock at the door. Malamine, being head of the house, went and opened it. It was Abdel Karim, escorted by three armed men. Within just a few seconds, the look on the doctor's face changed from serenity to surprise, from surprise to anger, and from anger to hatred.

"*Assalamu Aleikum*, Dr. Camara. I hope we aren't disturbing you."

"We were about to sit down for dinner, Captain."

"This won't take long."

"Why are you here, Captain?"

"Just patrol. We are still searching for information on the journal. You know . . ."

"Yes, I know."

"Have you read it?"

"I have. But you won't find it here. I opened it out of curiosity the day it was distributed in the city. But I left it where I found it. In front of the mosque."

"Now that's the attitude everyone in Kalep should adopt. Still, doctor, I have to go through with the search. I don't doubt your words, but it's the law. We did it with other families, and there is no reason that we wouldn't do it with yours. In fact, it would be unfair. Don't you agree?"

"Certainly."

"Good. So you will allow my men to enter and search your home. It will only take a few minutes. We've become used to it by now: we look for proof in the spots where traitors hide their evidence, thinking that they'll be able to evade the truth."

"Go ahead. There are no traitors here. But first . . ."

Abdel Karim was about to gesture to his men to come inside, but refrained and gave Malamine an odd look. Malamine stared at him in the same way he had back at the hospital during their first encounter, with hatred so intense he could barely conceal it. He spoke with a soft, broken voice which betrayed his feelings. The captain was amused by the effect he seemed to have on the doctor.

"Yes, doctor?"

"I'd like your men to leave their weapons outside. I have children, and one of them is still young."

"Oh, of course, doctor," the captain said with an unpleasantly sweet tone and in a voice that seemed very much unlike his own.

Then he gestured to the three men who had accompanied him. They laid their weapons down. Malamine moved aside. The patrol entered, followed by Abdel Karim and Malamine.

As soon as she recognized the voice of the captain of the Islamic police, Ndey Joor Camara asked Rokhaya to come close to her and told Idrissa to keep quiet. He remained seated on the couch, didn't move or turn around when the guards entered the house, and was seemingly indifferent to the unfolding events. Abdel Karim's men, as if completely oblivious to the family, headed straight into the other rooms of the house without making eye contact or saying a word. Two men stayed on the ground floor while the third went upstairs. Abdel Karim, preceding Malamine, walked toward the woman and her two kids.

"*Assalamu Aleïkum*, Adja."

"Good evening, Captain."

"I apologize for interrupting this important family time, but this won't take long. I promise."

Ndey Joor Camara glanced over the captain's shoulder and noticed her husband, fuming with anger. She smiled at him, as if trying to calm him down, before setting her eyes back on Abdel Karim, who continued to stare at her strangely.

"Do whatever you believe your job is, Captain."

"My duty, ma'am. My duty."

Ndey Joor didn't answer.

"Oh, now I see that you have a small child at home," Abdel Karim continued as he turned toward Malamine, who was now a few steps behind him. "She's very pretty, *Mashallah*. What's her name? What's your name, little one?"

Rokhaya turned her scared eyes toward her mother, at whose side she'd remained, as if asking her what to do. Ndey Joor simply placed her hand on the child's head and smiled.

"Don't be scared, sweetie."

"Oh, so you're scared of me. And why is that?" asked Abdel Karim.

Rokhaya gave the captain a look that only children know how to give adults: dreadful and accusatory.

"You're mean," said Rokhaya.

"Ah, really? And who told you that?"

"The kids on the street say it."

"Oh yeah? The kids? And why . . ."

"Captain, I ask that you please leave my daughter alone. She's just a child."

Abdel Karim turned back toward Malamine, who was still looking at him angrily, but now was no longer trying to conceal it. In fact, his anger seemed to be growing more intense by the minute. The captain scrutinized Malamine for a long while. A small grin grazed his lips, but Malamine didn't waver. Abdel Karim looked back toward Ndey Joor and the little girl. She was still staring at him with a mixture of juvenile hatred and fear, which gave her childlike face some charm.

"What did you do with Pothio? What did you do with the other dogs?" Rokhaya shouted.

Her question took everyone by surprise. The captain himself was taken aback. He opened his mouth a few seconds later to answer when Idrissa stood up suddenly and faced him. Up until then, he'd remained so still that Abdel Karim had failed to notice him.

"Ah, here we have the other child. I was wondering where he was. You are very discreet, my boy."

Idrissa said nothing and continued to stare at the captain.

Abdel Karim saw the same anger in his eyes that he noticed in Malamine's. But unlike his father, whose eyes were fuming with passion, the young boy's were intensely cold.

"Tell your men not to mess up any of my things please, Captain."

"It's already done, young man. The noises you hear aren't those of a ransack. We're used to searches, and we always put things back in their place."

"Very well."

He added nothing, grabbed a book from the shelf next to him, went back, sat on the couch, and began to read.

Abdel Karim brought his eyes back to Ndey Joor, thinking that her family was very strange.

Indeed, she seemed to be the only pillar of calm and peace in the house. Of all the eyes aimed at Abdel Karim, hers were the only ones devoid of hatred. Her husband's eyes harbored the brutal kind of hatred, her son's the chilling kind, and finally her daughter's the amusing kind. But Ndey Joor looked at him with compassion, pity almost, with gentle, calm, almost maternal eyes. He was taken aback once again but didn't look away.

Those eyes . . . he was certain he'd seen them somewhere before, perhaps when he was a child. He couldn't remember. And yet, when those eyes met his own, he had the clear yet strange impression that somebody had already looked at him that way, with the same unwavering calmness. But where? Who? Certainly not his mother, whose eyes were harsh and became lively only when she prayed or spoke of his father, who had died fighting for the Brotherhood. Eyes like his were small and lifeless. Maybe they were the eyes of one of his many aunts who had raised him as a child, but he couldn't tell for certain. He struggled to remember their faces. As for his grandmother's eyes, they were soft, but a softness that comes with age and proximity to death, a softness that was both melancholic and resigned: not these eyes. So where had he seen such a calm, composed, and reassuring gaze? Old flings? He had only loved once, a long time ago. She was the only woman he had ever loved. But he had suffered greatly. She had caused him so much pain that it was only through diligence and a herculean strength that he managed to forget her. He forgot her traits, her facial expressions, he erased her from his mind forever. She no longer held a place in his heart. She was but a lost, vague silhouette, like a shadow in the desert, like the mirage of an oasis. He no longer knew the face of the woman he had loved. That was before he decided to join the Brotherhood. Perhaps if she had loved him, he wouldn't be here now, standing in this house and wondering where he had seen such intriguing eyes before.

"Hey you! Stop looking at Mom like that!"

With the embarrassment that often comes when one is caught in the act, Abdel Karim looked at the little girl who had just dragged him out of his deep thoughts. He smiled at her, or maybe scowled, it wasn't clear. He then turned toward the side of the house where his men were making noise as they searched and instructed them to return.

"There's only the kitchen left, Captain," said one of them.

"Not necessary," said the captain as he turned toward the exit. "We're leaving."

"But maybe they have some in there," the oldest of the three objected.

"Yes," added another who looked like he was suffocating on his beard. "Remember yesterday, the family with the two copies in the kitchen under the fridge? Maybe . . ."

"We're leaving," said the captain again without turning around. His voice was calm and tough again.

The three men, while surprised, didn't think about protesting for a second and left quickly.

"I'm going to take my leave, doctor," he said turning toward Malamine, who seemed to have remained completely still since the patrol entered his house. "*Assalamu Aleïkum*, Adja Ndey Joor."

"Goodnight, Captain."

"Tell me, Adja Ndey Joor . . . I didn't even ask you how your back is doing."

"It's healing nicely."

"*Alhamdulillah*. Know that the responsible parties received the necessary punishment."

"That was not my wish. But you did your job, I suppose."

"My duty. Good night, children. I would have liked to know your name, though, little one."

Rokhaya scowled at him. Idrissa didn't react and continued to read his book calmly. The captain headed for the door to join his men, who were shaking with fear and waiting for him in the pickup.

Suddenly, a few feet from the door, he stopped as if he had been struck by lightning. Malamine, who was following, almost bumped into him.

"You forgot something, Captain?"

He didn't answer; he was stiff and stunned. His tall frame made him look ridiculous rather than impressive, like a fool shocked to see his reflection in the mirror for the first time.

"Is there a problem, Captain?" repeated Malamine.

"No . . . No. I was just looking at this photograph," he said, pointing to the frame hanging on the wall near the door. "It's a beautiful picture."

Then he left in a hurry, without adding anything else. Malamine slammed the door behind him.

CHAPTER 32

A lioune left the house of the woman whose young child he had cared for at the hospital a few weeks prior. The child was no longer in danger, running around happily once again on his skinny little legs, proudly showing off his bloated belly. His mother, eternally grateful to the young nurse, had invited him over for dinner, which Alioune had gladly accepted.

She was a good widow whose husband, a soldier, had been killed during the first battles between the army and the militia. Unable to leave, she remained in Kalep, hoping to join her husband's family in the capital one day. She had been waiting for this day for the last five years. In the meantime, she took on multiple jobs in order to feed and raise her son on her own. Alioune had sensed, in the way her voice lowered whenever she spoke of leaving, that she had perhaps subconsciously resigned herself to staying in Kalep forever. She no longer had hope that the province would one day be freed from the Islamists. She had even less hope that one day she might be able to leave with her son, given that her ties to this land were growing stronger every day. She lived modestly, renting out a small room in a large communal space managed by a wealthy businessman from the city, a friend of the Brotherhood. Alioune quickly noticed the room's remarkable tidiness, sometimes the only saving grace against poverty. Nevertheless, everything in the apartment, from the furniture to the clothing, the curtains to the sheets, the walls by the door and the windows, had clearly withstood the test of time, and also exposed the owner's deepest torments about the uncertainty of tomorrow. As the widow of a soldier killed in battle, she was entitled to a state pension which would have kept her out of poverty. It would have also prevented the State from being granted legal guardianship of her son. Unfortunately, these meager benefits were only accessible to widows living in the free zone; in other words, in the South. Those who had the misfortune of following their husbands up North, and the even greater misfortune of watching them die there, were left to fend for themselves. When the militia began attacking in the desert in order to take Kalep back from the military, her husband had entrusted her with all his savings "just in case," as if predicting his upcoming misfortune. He died the following day.

Alone and with limited means (her husband was only a corporal whose body was never found), she decided to leave the home she shared with her spouse. When the militia were at Kalep's doors, she moved into a small room in the south of the city, which she had thankfully been able to find on short notice. She had made the right choice: a few days later—after some violent battles from which Kalep still bore scars—the militia took over the city's military base. A few families remained in the camp thinking, optimistically, that their army would defeat the Brotherhood. All of them were robbed, beaten, and finally chased out of their homes by the jihadists who had taken over. They also took possession of a large part of the division's supplies (the crown jewel of the war's looting). In the haste of their departure, the division was forced to flee and leave many things behind: small firearms, assault rifles, boxes of ammunition, and even heavy weaponry which the jihadists were pleasantly surprised to find in their new stronghold. Nonetheless, Kalep's division had done what it could to push back. It was made up of around five hundred men, to be joined by around a thousand others at a later but unspecified date. The army was in charge of overseeing and supervising any movement on the Brotherhood's side and relaying that information to the military authorities. Said authorities had, with undeniable confidence, predicted that the Brotherhood was in fact too disorganized and spread out into small groups in the desert to be able to initiate a coherent and prolonged military attack. Five hundred men and another thousand on their way were deemed sufficient to secure a civil zone and push back—or perhaps even neutralize—a few amateur commandos in turbans in the heat of the desert, many of whom had never even held a firearm. The prophets were mistaken, as all prophets generally are, and Kalep was hit with a long, carefully organized attack. This attack was perhaps led by amateurs in turbans, but they were skilled, clever, disciplined, irrepressible, and unpredictable amateurs with acute knowledge of the land. The militia were experts at the art of war: from guerrilla warfare in the desert to attacks in the middle of the city, military booby traps—how many soldiers had lost their life or a limb by stepping on a landmine! From surprise raids to ambushes in the middle of the night, they had taken advantage of the soldiers of Kalep mentally and physically before landing a final blow—a long, violent, ruthless blow. Kalep's division was smaller in number, in equipment, poorly prepared, disorganized, and dominated tactically. After resisting for a lengthy period of time—three days, which arguably was more a result of their courage and sense of honor than any sort of skillful military tactic—they were forced to retreat toward the South.

The militia followed them and continued to push further southward, and as a result they were constantly conquering new territories in the North. They forced Kalep's army to retreat south many times. This was not something city officials liked to admit. After urgently decreed meetings between government officials, those potbellied triple-chinned men, comfortably settled in the headquarters' fancy armchairs, would send Kalep's people a swarm of brief but official statements, strange flyers, and reassuring messages. They mostly spoke about strategic withdrawals. Others, who were more pragmatic, more in tune with the appropriate language of crisis, more familiar with military laconism, would refer to "retreats" instead. It was more mysterious, more ambiguous, less obvious. More militaristic. More in line with esprit de corps and less damaging for troop morale. During this time, the army fled, withdrew, fell back, retreated. The orders they received were as numerous as they were conflicting, often followed by hazardous strategies dictated by some high ranking, all-knowing beings. They tried desperate forms of retaliation, turning those who participated into cannon fodder, always hoping for reinforcements, reinforcements that were always on the way, but never came. They scoured the sky, which never delivered any of the promised aerial reinforcements. After just about ten days of battle, Kalep's division was reduced to two hundred and sixty-eight men. They tried their hardest to mitigate the extent of their failures by killing as many men as possible on the enemy's side to claim some small, quickly forgotten victories. The militia—it was unclear exactly how many were in their ranks, between two and four thousand according to certain official reports—lost ninety-three men, based on official estimates.

After two weeks, the Brotherhood took hold of the entire Bandiani province and was preparing to take the center of the country. It was the perfect stronghold to later capture the South, the capital of Sumal, and, finally, the entire country. At the beginning of the third week, when Kalep's two hundred remaining soldiers were about to surrender Baka, one of the country's main and more central cities, to the Brotherhood, reinforcements finally arrived. The cavalry made its way, the air force poured in. Rows of men came to the rescue, accompanied by triumphant military tunes, and finally Sumal's army was able to push back the militia. They had nevertheless lost the North. The battles took place a few hundred miles north of Baka, in a zone that became the imaginary border between an Islamic North on one side, and the Center and free South on the other. While the army was able to resist and push back enemy attacks quite easily, they had a hard time gaining ground in the North. It was safe to say their enemy was strong and well positioned. After some months of respite, the battles became rarer, ceasing entirely for some time before starting up again. Each side seemed content, at least temporarily, with its respective positions and gains. They observed each other, all the while polishing their weapons and strategies in anticipation of a final battle which everyone seemed to both expect and dread at the same time. The border would sway, sometimes a few miles in one direction, other times in the other, giving more or less advantage to either side. But, realistically, it never changed. Negotiations were out of the question: Sumal's government was firm in its conviction that "we do not negotiate with terrorists" in order to justify its decisions. The Brotherhood had no such mantra; theirs was simpler: to do God's work until death.

This had been going on for four years.

For four years, Fanta Soumaré, Alioune's host, had been living with the hypothetical hope that the city would one day be freed and that she would be able to go and live with her in-laws in the capital. For four years, rumors of a decisive attack had circulated at least once a week amongst the people of Kalep. For four years, these rumors consistently proved to be false. For four years, the State had promised to free the occupied territories as quickly as possible, and promised swift and decisive action. After four years she had given up, deciding that she was better off focusing her energy on survival rather than hope.

In spite of all this, Fanta had been fairly happy all evening long. Her son's recovery had put a smile back on her face. She prepared a delicious couscous for Alioune, whom she now referred to as her "son's savior." Of course, she didn't let the man know that she had gone into debt just to buy a good piece of meat, but Alioune figured as much. So they had both lied to each other out of sheer modesty.

* * *

Despite everything, Alioune still believed that Kalep was a beautiful city, one that he enjoyed wandering at night. Naturally, some things had been destroyed, ransacked, burnt, and never rebuilt; and of course, the atmosphere—which is the greatest measure of a city's character—had changed since the arrival of the Islamists. It was true that people no longer went out after nightfall, that Kalep's carefree spirit had been replaced by fear and suspicion. These days, the city, which had once been joyous and bursting with life, was covered by a strict veil of religion.

Alioune was the first one to admit this. His walks felt different. The same streets that had once been filled with cheerful cries, laughs, exclamations, with distant sounds of celebrations and music resonating from the nightclubs, were now empty, and Alioune walked alone in absolute silence. From time to time, he would encounter other shy silhouettes draped in shadows. Kalep, with its deserted streets, had become a sad place. And while some cities are graced with newfound lyrical charm when night falls, Kalep was not one of those. It couldn't pride itself on its desolation and stillness, because the city was beautiful only when immersed in constant noise. Alioune recognized that for this reason, the city was no longer the same. Like nature, Kalep's nights abhorred emptiness and silence. That night, he felt a strange sensation wandering the vast alleys which, once abundant and cheery, were now cold and even calmly threatening. Kalep's streets were built for a human tide, for shouting and loud voices, for honking and harmless mischief; to remove this was to rob them of their charm. Unlike some other places, Kalep was not a city whose silent nights gave it an aura of pleasant mystery. On the contrary, Kalep lived off its noises and through them, through its scents, and through its people. Once the streets became deserted, Kalep was nothing more than a ghost town. The big streets lost their majesty, and their emptiness became almost absurd. The avenues extended endlessly, completely overwhelming the solitary stroller. Even the side streets, whose sudden openings, unexpected and delicious detours, and unknown bends never ceased to offer surprises, were rendered boring and grey: they all began to look the same. Now that the streets were no longer beaten by the people's expansive, customary footsteps, the charm that sometimes comes with age was lost, the city's energy and joy along with it.

Alioune wandered the streets slowly, aimlessly. The Brotherhood had taken hold of the city, robbed it of all its joy, and left it barren, silent, and devoid of adventure. Out of loyalty and respect, however, he continued to go on walks regularly, searching for hidden beauty amongst the ruins. Kalep shivered. The night was cool without being cold and the moon was softly veiled; the city drowned in morbid beauty, in apathy. Kalep's spirit and splendor were gone. Its trees, which were large and scattered throughout, stiff and soaring toward the sky, offered the city some welcome shade during the day. Their outlines and dense foundations made them look like a marching army of giants, or perhaps of sublime martyrs in their surrender. That was the spirit of Kalep tonight: like an imprisoned mistress who wept because she had been abandoned by her lovers for far too long. Alioune was one of the few who still dared to walk around at night, a thought that gave him a sense of peace. He felt as loyal as a dog with his tongue out and his tail wagging. He had been walking for a long time, without a word, absorbed in a silent dialogue with this dying city. He was searching for beauty and believed that, despite everything, Kalep was still capable of offering it to him.

It was true that in spite of what the Brotherhood had done, there was something that it would never be able to kill in this city: its memory. The memory of the city as it used to be, filled with old noises, with murmurs of rainstorms five years past, with the invigorating laughs and the ever-present smells. All of these things, the *had-beens* of Kalep, its memory, would never disappear, at the very least not as long as the people refused to forget them. He believed that this was where the real battle was. Every war, in his eyes, was a war for memory, in other words a war that must be fought in the name of the survival of memory. War seemed like a perpetual attempt to erase the past, a vast destruction of cities, but more importantly the destruction of something even more essential to man: the memory of what he used to be, his joys, his hopes, of happier times. That's what we must refuse to forget at all costs. And not forgetting is continuing to see, to search for, to find, amidst the silence and grayness, the pieces of these memories. It could be in a street or on a bench, on a sidewalk or by the square where the markets are held. Whether these places still existed or not mattered little; what mattered was that they remained alive in the mental landscape of each individual man, from the perspective of his singular experience and intimate memories. Like a painting, with all its colors, its textures, its landscape— this is what needed to live on. For Alioune, every war involved both fighting a machine whose sole purpose was the destruction of memory, and fighting against our own internal tendency to forget. Every time he walked around the city and remembered old times, he became overwhelmed with the feeling that he was fighting back better than anyone could with weapons or violence. To be at war was, at least for him, to refuse the mutilation of memory caused by the constant feeling of unhappiness, fear, and desperation. Nostalgia is not fatally tinted by sadness. Once it's stripped of regret, melancholy, and bitterness, only lightness remains. And if nothing else gets in the way, when there is only lightness, the extraordinary density of happier times returns.

Alioune was sure of it: if a war could ever be considered "lovely,"[30] it was only because it enabled the revival of happy memories. Death has but one hunting ground: life. And so life is where we must confront it—in the present, at the heart of existence, fighting for the preservation of memory.

[30] "Oh God! What a lovely war!" Guillaume Apollinaire, *L'Adieu du cavalier* (trans. Anne Hyde Greet).

CHAPTER 33

Exhausted and unable to fall asleep, Malamine headed to the living room to read He hoped that maybe a few pages would tire him enough to plunge him into a slumber as deep as his wife's. He grabbed a book at random from one of the shelves—he always let fate decide his reading—then sat cross-legged on the carpet.

He was reading but understood nothing: the sentences, words, paragraphs, the page, the text in its entirety, everything was flickering, swirling and blending before his eyes, forming a shapeless, grayish, dark jumble which caused him to become dizzy. He read the same sentence for a while, because every time he reached the end of the line, he would systematically start again and ponder it without understanding. It seemed absurd to him. In truth, what he didn't realize was that the sentence didn't end at the end of the line, and that to really grasp its meaning, he'd have had to read the following line, too. But he had forgotten that he had to move on to the next line.

Eventually, he closed the book and sat in the same position on the floor, his head between his hands. The evening's events had exhausted him; he simultaneously felt the sadness caused by the conversation with his son, the loneliness that nagged at him (but whose origin he didn't know), the fear of not being up to the tasks he had yet to accomplish, and the extreme anger prompted by Abdel Karim's unexpected visit. It surprised him how much hatred he felt for this man; it was as if the mere fact of him being there, of seeing him was enough to turn Malamine into someone else, a stranger to himself, to his own body and emotions.

But the real reason for his insomnia was the conversation he'd had with Idrissa.

He had been too weak to bring up the topic which, for all these years, had been slowly tearing them apart. He could not say anything about Ismaïla, the one who had separated them. It was precisely around the time of his departure that he began to feel his younger son's distance. And once again he, Malamine, was the one responsible for all of this: for Idrissa's growing solitude, for the increasing distance between them, for everything. Ismaïla had left, and that was also his fault. Idrissa deserved explanations that Malamine had never found the courage or strength to give him. And yet this is all he wanted: to concede to him that it was his fault. And that he knew it.

* * *

It all started five years earlier. The Brotherhood was still in the desert. Despite the rumors of an imminent attack by the Islamists and increasing nervousness among the troops, Kalep was still a fairly bustling city and, more importantly, it was still free. Rokhaya had just turned four, Idrissa was twelve, and Ismaïla was seventeen. He was becoming a man. But Malamine and Ndey Joor weren't happy: they were worried about their eldest's condition. For two years—in other words, since the age of fifteen—Ismaïla had spoken to almost no one, locked himself in his room frequently, and was losing weight alarmingly fast. He was not miserable, or even just sad: he was a smiling young man, polite, funny, and witty. Those characteristics would spring back up intact every time he emerged from his solitude to participate in the family's everyday affairs, as if he'd never lost them, and as if he'd never been affected by his mysterious and sudden asceticism. Initially, Ndey Joor and

Malamine were not too alarmed by this, thinking maybe his propensity for solitude stemmed from a newfound passion: they knew of his love for literature and assumed perhaps he had taken on reading more intensely, or that maybe he had started writing, which would explain why he would lock himself in his room more frequently. But this behavior wasn't short-lived. It lasted weeks, then months, then finally an entire year. At first, they didn't ask him what he was doing. They preferred to leave him to his own devices hoping that, one day, he would open up to them. Ismaïla didn't. When he came home from school—it was during the time that the French school was still open—or during vacation, or any time that the family was together, he would behave normally, laughing, joking around, listing off a few nice words. But he never spoke of what he did in his room for hours on end, as if he himself was unaware of his strange behavior.

A whole year went by. Truthfully, Malamine and Ndey Joor were more curious than they were worried.

Then Ismaïla turned sixteen. It was at that time that things really took a turn for the worse.

Ismaïla lost his appetite, spoke even less, locked himself in his room more often, and signs of long sleepless nights appeared on his face. His eyes became red, his somber and tired gaze disclosed his internal torments, which were reinforced by the appearance of wrinkles on his forehead.

In just a year, he had aged. Visibly worn out by his sleepless nights, he began to miss his alarm more often, to skip entire days of school; his teachers, who had always regarded him highly, grew worried. They expressed their concerns to Malamine and Ndey Joor. When they finally spoke to their son about it, he said nothing, and simply listened in silence with a dazed look on his face. Up until then, the only thing left that made him nice to be around was his natural joyfulness, and even that had ultimately faded after a few months. Ismaïla became aphasic and grim. One would look at him and feel as though a veil was covering his eyes. They were turned inwards, and would only focus on the mysterious and secretive internal experience he had confined himself to. His physical transformation intensified, mirroring that of his soul: an ominous glimmer appeared in his tired eyes; he let his beard grow and his skinny shoulders began to sag. Soon, he wore only long tunics which went all the way down to his ankles, giving him a ghost-like appearance. He no longer laughed. Idrissa, with whom he had been very close, began to look at him with fear. How many times had he tried to enter Ismaïla's room to get a peek into what was happening, only to be chased off at the doorway by a frigid gaze, harsh bullying, or even a sudden gesture? His room remained closed, inaccessible to all, even to his mother, who had not seen it in months. At first, they thought that perhaps he was engaging in some illicit consumption or even trafficking, but it wasn't the case: Ismaïla had always been asthmatic and allergic to all types of smoke, especially from cigarettes. As for being a criminal or a smuggler, he would have had to be social and well known. He'd been confined to his solitude for a year, no longer seeing or interacting with anyone, no longer interested in those around him, not even his friends, who became spectators of his metamorphosis. They confirmed that he was always alone at school, too, with a strange look on his face, sitting at the back of the room or in a corner of the school's courtyard. His friends added that Ismaïla's only companions were some strange books that he tried to conceal with great effort whenever anyone approached him.

Ismaïla changed so drastically in such a short time that Ndey Joor and Malamine were too caught off guard to react. This was perhaps their first mistake, the first of many. If they had known how to react from the start, maybe they could've fought the evil at its root. But they couldn't do it. They didn't know how. Trouble had come to light and grown insidiously under their gaze, visible yet intangible like a ghost, obvious but also hidden and devious.

By the time Malamine had spoken with his wife and made the decision to act, it was probably too late.

One day, he decided to go pick up his son from school. He wanted them to speak alone, far from the worried or fearful gazes of his family. He suggested they walk toward the cemetery, one of the city's calmest areas. They walked in silence as Malamine silently rehearsed what he was going to say to his son, who was still closed off, his beard bushy, his eyes sunken in their sockets. He was dressed in a gloomy black robe which made him look like a gravedigger. It was during this walk that Malamine understood, perhaps more than ever before, the extent of his son's transformation. When he was still a child, even up until the age of twelve, the two of them had come here on walks. This was how they bonded: they played, chatted, Ismaïla would ask questions appropriate to his age, or ask for advice with girls, or tell his father that he would one day be a teacher and teach kids how to be responsible, and many other things that now seemed so distant. The teenager walking alongside him had become a stranger.

They approached the cemetery when he began to speak:

"Ismaïla, I need to speak to you seriously."

"I'm listening, Father."

"Your mother and I are worried. Everyone is worried about you. Your brother, your friends, your teachers. Even your younger sister who is only three is scared of you. Your mother and I are also scared. But not of you. For you."

He didn't answer and continued to walk, his head lowered. The second Malamine started to wonder if he had in fact heard him, his son began to speak. His voice seemed different, as if the words it spoke were not his own, as if his voice had been muted for so long that it no longer knew how to speak. It was a deaf, hoarse, possessed voice. It scared Malamine.

"I don't see why I'm worrying you, Father. I am doing very well, *Alhamdulillah*. God watches over me and I thank Him for it. I really don't see what is causing you to be so worried."

"Are you pretending not to want to understand what I'm saying, or not to see it? Are you the only one who doesn't realize that you're destroying yourself? Your mother and I can't take this anymore. We can't continue like this, doing nothing when you seem to be slowly dying, locked up in your room. Look at yourself. Your current state. Your body, your clothes. You seem . . . You seem dead . . ."

"It's not true, Father . . ."

"Ismaïla, how dare you . . . ?"

"I ask that you not interrupt me, Father. I respect you, just as I respect every other one of God's creatures on earth. But God has commanded us to tell the truth, and what you say is not the truth. You're judging me based on my exterior. Do you not know that interior life is far more important? Do you fail to recognize the benefits of meditation, of divine contemplation? You must think, you must all think for that matter, that I'm going crazy, or that all of this is consuming me. You think I don't see you. But I see you. Don't think that just because I've been living out my faith and trying to become closer to God, I've become blind to your stares, those fearful gazes that look at me as if I had the plague, your apprehensive attitudes, your whispers. Do you really fear the man who turns himself internally to God and dedicates his life to Him? Why are those who aspire to the Truth shunned, feared, hated?"

He could say nothing. His son continued.

"You think I'm destroying myself. On the contrary, I've never been so strong and at peace with myself. I am a servant and slave of Allah. Nothing can destroy me except the Will of Allah. You should not worry for me, I'm in God's hands, just as you are, just as everyone on earth is."

"But what happened to you, Ismaïla?"

"I was saved."

"By whom? Who saved you? Who put these things in your head? You're still too young for these things . . ."

"Allah's Love has no age. The purity of one's heart is not an adult matter. It's not only for the elderly or for children. Faith is a fire that can light up all hearts and save all lives."

"Who spoke to you of this? Who?"

"None other than Allah Himself, Father. He spoke to me, I heard Him in my heart."

His voice grew louder, vibrated, and there was a twinkle in his eye. He seemed, in that very moment, to have come back to life, but a different life, animated by different fires.

"Ismaïla, think about your future, your mother."

"I think about the Lord, Father. That's my future, I have no other."

"Do you realize what you're doing? You're throwing away your future for things you don't understand . . ."

"Supposing I don't understand them, whose fault is that? What did you teach me about God? What did you teach me, you, Father, about religion, other than a few verses that I would just recite mechanically to pray? That's not real understanding. To recite the divine word without understanding it, to regurgitate it without grasping its truth, its beauty, its fire, its passion, its love, what is that other than sin? Again, what have you taught me about God? What have you told me of Him? Answer, Father, answer. What have you taught me? You say that you're Muslim and that you adore God. What have you told me that was truthful? Did you ever talk to me about salvation? About the Quran? The prophet? The meaning of prayer? Do you really know any of these things, or are you just behaving like the thousands who pretend to be believers but are merely shadows, people who perform acts but are incapable of grasping their underlying truth and beauty? Yes, that's it. You cheat. You pretend. You imitate. You don't even really know what it means to pray, not any more than you know how to read the Quran or to be a true Muslim. You have no internal strength as a Muslim, and God is as much a stranger to you as all those Muslims that you think of as brothers. You're all lying, and your sins are all the more serious when you make them . . ."

He hit him. He couldn't help it. Ismaïla continued, without ever losing his cool.

"You can hit me as much as you like. The truth of what I'm sharing with you will hurt you even more than any slaps you can give me."

"I'm sorry, Ismaïla, I . . ."

"I forgave you the moment you raised your hand. I prayed for you because I know what motivates you. Anger, the instrument of Sheïtan. It threatens us every day at every moment, and it's difficult to resist it except if you build an internal fortress, one protected by God."

He stopped, turned his face toward the sky, closed his eyes, and prayed. The shadows started to stretch out over the ground. Malamine stayed there, watching him as if he no longer recognized him. Was this still his son? Where had he gone? The one who used to go on walks with him? Where did he go? When did he leave? Why hadn't he stopped him? When Malamine looked at his son in that moment, turned toward the sky, he felt as if he'd already lost him.

"Ismaïla . . ."

When he looked at his father again, his face was drenched in tears.

"Ismaïla, you're crying . . ."

"The joys that Allah provides can be measured only in tears. I am a happy and serene man, Father. And I will stay this way, Father, whether you like or not. This is my present and my future. God is my life."

"Don't do this, my son . . ."

"It's already done, by the Grace of Allah. Join me. Come."

"It could kill your mother . . ."

"Stop annoying me with my mother. I've made my choice. Respect it and she will respect it also."

"You're losing yourself, son. I can't remain indifferent to all of this. I'm your father. If that still means anything to you and if you have any respect or consideration left for me, obey me and abandon these dark paths that you've set yourself on."

"What? How dare you . . ."

"I'm not questioning your devotion. It's a noble path, and if your heart calls you to follow this path then I have no right to stop you. But if your love of God makes you forget your love for your own, then becoming religious is a crime. To love God is to love men, and not to separate yourself from them."

"Who speaks of no longer loving you? On the contrary, I turn to Allah to better love you, to better save you."

"But you're turning away from your family and you don't even realize it. You don't speak anymore, you don't say hello, you don't notice our presence, you don't eat anymore. Is that a way to love those who never stopped loving you?

"The path toward the Lord is a long and solitary one. But I'm not forgetting you. When the time comes, you will be with me."

"You are still young. You don't know what it means."

"I know perfectly well what it means. What do you think I've dedicated myself to in the last few months? To reading. To learning. To understanding. I study Arabic, I read entire treatises on theology, I read the Quran, I understood every one of its verses. I memorized the Sunnah, and I learned thousands of Hadiths, I meditated."

"Look where it has led you. This is not what God's love does."

"But it contributes to it."

"Look at yourself, you don't seem happy. And yet happiness is what we should feel when we grow closer to God."

"You're still judging me based on my appearance, Father. My heart overflows with joy."

"You've changed, Ismaïla. You disappoint me tremendously."

"I've changed paths. You should be proud that I turned myself toward God."

"Not in this way."

"There is no other."

He spit at his feet and walked away. From that day on, Malamine no longer spoke to or looked at his eldest son. That was his second mistake.

The months that followed were difficult. The atmosphere at home was becoming increasingly painful to bear in addition to the one in the city, which was just as heavy, riddled and poisoned with rumors. The garrison's ever more frequent movements foreshadowed the Islamists' looming presence in the desert. The potential of an attack, the anticipation of a battle, and the uncertainty of tomorrow, combined with the government's vague proposals, only added to the confusion of an increasingly untenable and unpredictable situation.

As a precaution, many families had left Kalep for the center or south of the country. A sort of psychosis settled in, slowing down and contaminating all of Kalep's services.

Malamine and Ndey Joor had discussed the possibility of leaving Kalep, but his work held him back: asking for a transfer would be a long process, and almost certainly unsuccessful. After so many migrations, the government had begun refusing to allow high-ranking public servants to leave the Bandiani province, which would only weaken it further. So they had decided to stay in Kalep no matter what.

Their relationship with Ismaïla was not improving. Since their conversation, Malamine no longer spoke to him, he ignored him entirely, leaving Ndey Joor to try and reason with their eldest. But Ismaïla was not any more receptive to his mother's arguments than he was to his father's. In truth, the situation was worsening. Ismaïla no longer made any efforts to be sociable, he stopped going to school—which half of the teachers had left—and locked himself in his room for days on end, leaving only to eat, do his ablutions, and use the bathroom. Sometimes he wouldn't eat for an entire day. Malamine was sad to see the suffering this caused Ndey Joor and the kids. Propelled by her unwavering maternal instinct, she tried to talk to Ismaïla every day, but he wouldn't listen. She also tried to talk to her husband, desperately trying to convince him to stop ignoring his son and make an effort to help him. But his pride and anger were too strong. He continued to ignore Ismaïla, who, by the way, never seemed to take notice. His younger son, Idrissa, seemed completely lost and looked at his brother with incomprehension and distress. The situation saddened him. He saw two men with whom he was very close and alongside whom he had grown up turn their backs on each other. He asked for help, for an explanation, for reassurance, and attempted many cries for help, all of which went unanswered. His mother was too busy trying to save Ismaïla and convince Malamine not to abandon him. Malamine's contempt for Ismaïla, was so great that he had trouble even talking about it. His third mistake was thinking Idrissa wanted to address what was happening with his older brother: what he really wanted, though, was less about getting an explanation and more about feeling reassured, comforted, and less alone in all of this. But that never happened. The situation went on. Ismaïla entered his seventeenth year.

One night, the drama unfolded.

They had just finished dinner in a persistent and heavy silence, one they'd gotten used to in recent months, when Ndey Joor burst into tears. She couldn't bear the situation for another second. She sobbed heavily, completely unresponsive to Malamine's efforts to calm her. She yelled that it was unfair, that God was out to get her and her family, that she didn't know what she had done to deserve all this, and that she would rather die than live with a family where father and son no longer speak. Her breakdown was sudden, frightening, and lengthy; it grew more intense as it went on. Malamine didn't know what to do. Ndey Joor began to scream, to shout, to rip her hair out. The children were there, startled and afraid. Only Ismaïla remained apathetic, observing his mother's hysterical outburst calmly. Malamine remembered Rokhaya. She was crying, clinging to Idrissa, who was terrified and alternated between looking at his mother, at his father, and at Ismaïla, who was next to him but didn't move. Soon, Ndey Joor was overtaken by violent convulsions and fainted into Malamine's arms. Initially distraught, he looked around for help and only saw his kids. Idrissa and Rokhaya were petrified. Ismaïla was stoic. Malamine looked at him for a few seconds and then, after regaining some strength, he spoke to him for the first time in many months.

"Help me carry your mother to her bed. I'll take care of her. Idrissa, take care of your sister. Go upstairs and stay there until I come get you."

Idrissa and Rokhaya obeyed. Ismaïla hadn't moved. Malamine had already grabbed Ndey Joor under her arms, and was waiting for his son to pick her up by the legs. But Ismaïla still hadn't moved.

"What are you waiting for? I told you to help me carry your mother to bed."

"I don't know if I can."

He thought perhaps he had misheard.

"Excuse me?"

This time he looked at him with confusion.

"I don't know if I can," repeated Ismaïla with the same degree of calmness.

"If you can what?"

"If I can help you carry Mom, if I can touch her . . ."

"What do you mean if you can touch her?"

His level of incomprehension led to fear and even anger.

"I don't know if I can. For some time now, I've decided I no longer want to engage in any physical contact with women. But I don't know if that applies to my own mother. I'm not sure . . ."

Malamine was so dumbfounded that he nearly dropped Ndey Joor, whose head almost hit the ground violently. He no longer recognized his son at all; he was disgusted, repulsed, and was overtaken by a sudden need to throw up. Ismaïla didn't move. His arms dangled alongside his body, his unwavering eyes stared at his father, his entire silhouette exuded a composure so intense it was unbearable.

"Ismaïla, she's . . ."

He wasn't able to finish his sentence. Tears streamed down his face at the same time as his nausea overwhelmed him. He threw up next to his wife's body, but not far enough to avoid getting any on her face. It came out in jolts, in strong and painful torrents. He had the feeling that with every one of them his intestines were twisting so much that they would rupture.

"She's my mother, I know. But I don't know if I can, I haven't read anything on the subject."

At that moment, Malamine felt a hand on his shoulder. Idrissa had come back down, worried by the noise that his father had made when he threw up.

"Go back up and take care of your sister, Idrissa, everything is fine. As for you, get out of my house and never come back. I banish you, I curse you, I despise you. Get out and go live with your God. I don't want to see you anymore, you're no longer my son. Go to your room, take your things, and get out of here. Get out of our lives. You're not a part of them anymore."

He remembered that he had said this calmly. His throat

hurt, his stomach too. He had saliva dangling from his mouth and foam at the corner of his lips.

"Dad, no, not that, I . . ."

"I told you to go upstairs, Idrissa. This man is no longer your brother. He's leaving."

That was his fourth mistake.

"I thank the Lord for making things easier," said Ismaïla as his brother was going back upstairs. "I was going to leave the house one day or another regardless. I'm going to the desert. I will join the Brotherhood. I want to be a part of the Brotherhood. That's my destiny, because that's where God is."

"Go where you like. But get out and don't come back ever again."

"It's unfortunate that things have to end this way. But if this is the will of God, I'll accept it."

Malamine didn't answer. Instead, he simply looked at him with contempt. He then carried his wife on his shoulders, turned his back to the man facing him, and went toward their room. Before going inside, he heard his son's voice.

"Goodbye, Dad. May Allah keep you and watch over you all. Tell Mom I love her."

Malamine walked inside the room without turning back. That was the last time he saw his eldest son, who then embraced Idrissa and kissed Rokhaya's forehead goodbye before leaving. She was in tears, terrified.

When Ndey Joor awoke a few hours later, Malamine told her what had happened. She cried until dawn.

Two days after Ismaïla's departure, the army installed barbed wire along the desert's border to ward off the fundamentalist threat. It was too late.

They received no news for an entire year. No sign of life. Ismaïla had left. They looked for him among those who took Kalep and chased the army, they asked a few soldiers and showed them his photo: nothing worked. Ismaïla had simply vanished in the desert. Did he die in the first battles? Perish in the desert? Had he been transferred to another branch of the Brotherhood in a different country? One after the other, they got used to the idea that he was probably dead.

And it was Malamine who had killed him. The guilt never left him, and never would. If Ismaïla had left and died, he was mainly responsible. That's why Idrissa looked at him that way.

CHAPTER 34

One never truly measures the extent to which every war is also, perhaps mainly, an initiative of destruction through the manipulation of language. Words are distorted to comply with people's passions and used as rhetoric to express conflicting goals, which are all still alike in their allegiance to violence.

Because every war is a manipulation of language, or worse, its absolute alienation, it ultimately becomes a fundamental attack on Truth.

CHAPTER 35

In the name of God, the All Merciful, the All Compassionate.

The day is coming to an end and I still have not found the authors of the journal. They're well-hidden and they're careful. Neither the interrogations nor the surprise searches have helped us catch them, not even the threats of retaliation against the province, in other words against the public good. This game will last longer than originally anticipated. I rejoice in this fact, obviously; in my eyes, the Lord's challenges become all the more valuable when they are difficult. We will find these heretics. I will find them and I will punish them. What does it matter if Kalep's people cooperate or not, report them or not, protect them or betray them; what do I care if they know their identities or not? I'll find them alone if I must. I've already made a vow, and I'm repeating it here. May God be my witness.

I will act soon.

I'm still surprised, however, at how calm the people are despite the threats and the promises of rewards. Whose side are they on? They still act on their instincts, and that's dangerous. Sometimes it happens that everything we believed we had ignited in each citizen, be it his faith, fervor, passion, or love for God, dissipates, simply cracks, gets blown away by the wind, crumbles, dries out the in same way a snake's skin dries out after its molt. In these moments, the masses seem to forget everything and think only of their own selfish interests.

Therein lies the danger. It's one we must always be wary of, even when it seems to have been successfully tamed.

* * *

Nevertheless, something extraordinary happened earlier tonight. Now I know. I know why I had the feeling that I'd met this woman before, why I had the feeling that I had already seen her. I know where my discomfort comes from. It's her eyes. I've seen them before. They're engraved in my memory. How can I forget such a gaze? Now I know that she's his mother.

Adjaratou Ndey Joor Camara is Ismaïla Camara's mother. I'm sure.

It was perhaps too obvious for me to make the connection before today: sometimes, when lights are too close to one another, they transform clarity of the mind into total blindness. All I had to do was think, rummage through my memory, concentrate. But surely, I was too taken aback by this woman's gaze to really contemplate the origin of my confusion. I know it now, and I was so surprised by it earlier that I worry Doctor Camara, or worse, Ndey Joor herself, may have noticed my astonishment. This woman's eyes are the same as Ismaïla's. I'm certain of it.

Ismaïla is the one I saw earlier in the photograph hanging in the Camaras' home. He's the one I saw smiling, his arm on his father's shoulder. There's no doubt in my mind. After all, how could I ever forget that young man's face?

Ismaïla . . . Ismaïla and his ghostly aura. Ismaïla and his eyes lost in the sky. Ismaïla and his gaze, his mystery, his impertinent youth, his faith, his knowledge. He flew in and out of my life as a shooting star flies across a clear night sky during the dry season. This is the reason I'll never forget him. And if I didn't recognize him immediately in his mother it's because it seemed so incongruous to me that he might still have family alive. Not for a second could I have imagined that this family even existed, may God be my witness. Ismaïla always seemed to be alone, without any sort of attachment, tucked away in his terrible and well-kept solitude.

He seemed to appear out of nowhere, as if he had been birthed by a dune in the desert the very same day that I saw him for the first time. We were camping a few hundred miles to the north of Kalep. I had just been named head of the Islamic Police and we were starting to train for the decisive attack on Kalep and the rest of the province. We'd had a few military victories and completed a few operations which were quick and unpredictable enough to destabilize Kalep's troops and lower their morale. Our men were confident. God was with us and showing us the way every day. After years of hiding out in the desert, years of building an army worthy of fighting a holy war, years of recruiting and training men who had never held weapons in their life, we were finally ready. Victory was promised to us. Kalep's soldiers were brave, but not numerous enough and surely overconfident. We were certain we would win. They came back empty-handed from their expeditions in the desert: we dominated these vast expanses better than they did, we tolerated the heat better than they did, we protected each other from its mirages and mystery better than they could. The desert was our home, and we had lived there for so long that not a single square inch of it was foreign to us. Slowly, patiently, surely, we marched on Kalep. Neither Sumal's military authorities nor the lookouts had seen anything, or if they had, they had simply dismissed it. That's how we were able to reach the city gates, which would open the province up to us, then the country, and finally the entire subregion. The hearts of our men were animated by a fever, a mixture of fear and excitement that always precedes great battles; God's fire shone through their eyes. One of our men needed only to look at one of his brothers in order to feel the reassurance of a guaranteed victory. Just as God had guided the prophet and his companions to victory against the unbelievers in order to protect the holy land, so He guided us toward swift and decisive victory. We were only beginning our preparations when the atmosphere began to fill with that certain aura suited to beautiful death. Our campsite was buzzing: we were polishing our weapons, practicing our shots, perfecting our tactics; Allahu Akbars could be heard frequently, echoing from voice to voice. Collective prayers turned into moments of sheer gratitude. Hundreds of our brothers came together, united and strong like large walls held together by the cement of faith, not only preparing to push back the invaders—but rather to destroy them. We were confident. And I, always skeptical and reserved in nature, was starting to share their enthusiasm. I was beginning to believe in our collective success.

That's when Ismaïla arrived. He appeared one day on top of a dune, where a division that I was in charge of was training. He walked toward us, slowly, and we watched him come forward, almost hypnotized. He looked like a mirage, a demonic vision, like a desert's well-kept secret. And he walked toward us. The sun was blinding, and its vapors often blurred our sight. For a few seconds, his distant silhouette seemed to disappear. For a moment, I myself believed that it had perhaps just been a mirage. Had my skepticism not been tested over the years in this same desert? One of my men even aimed with his weapon. I stopped him: we didn't have any ammunition to waste on a ghost. A single man was heading toward us. We waited. The silhouette sharpened, then finally reached us. It was Ismaïla.

Only his feet were visible, peeking out below his long black caftan. He was wearing leather sandals reminiscent of the ancient Romans. He carried a backpack and nothing more. Though his face had been marked and burned by the sun, there was still a sense of youth about him—which his beard, which could only have started growing two years prior, was trying to conceal. I realized immediately that this was a boy. But when he spoke, his voice was mature, deep, a man's voice.

He explained to us very simply that he wanted to enlist in the Brotherhood, to serve it. His request didn't surprise us: he was not the first boy to join us to fight for our cause. But he was different from the others, perhaps in his intentions. Most of our recruits joined us for the usual reasons: some of them were lost and looking for a substitute family; others, often former bandits, were looking for a form of redemption and a way to shrug off their former lives in religion; some felt robbed and wanted to fight against the State; and then there were those who were simply drawn to the idea of holding a weapon in their hands and the feeling of invincibility that often comes with brandishing it and arbitrarily deciding to shoot. All of them saw a family in the Brotherhood, a new collective entity where they might be able to rebuild their identities.

Few came to search for God. To really search for him. Few considered the Brotherhood as a spiritual experience, as an internal quest, as a test of faith. A lot of them were drawn to the organization, to the weapons, to the militia's power; few were able to truly grasp what it represented, the strength of spirit it was able to offer. I was one of these chosen few, and had met only two others like myself before that day. Ismaïla was the third. We only had to exchange a few words for me to understand that.

Obviously, joining the Brotherhood was a highly selective process, so I put him to the test. In order to be accepted, candidates had to meet certain requirements: knowing how to recite the Quran, how to give reports from the Hadiths, how to pray correctly, and how to talk about faith. There was a time when meeting these qualifications was unavoidable, and when the Brotherhood turned away many young men who tried to enroll without any knowledge of religion. Sadly, because we had to grow our army, the selection process became less demanding and an increasing number of ignoramuses—barely more educated than nonbelievers—managed to join the Brotherhood. The authorities wanted it this way: they needed to get men first, they would worry about coaching them later. I myself had contributed to the moral, intellectual, and Islamic training of most of the men under my command. But when the time came to pass the exams, it became obvious to me that they were just dreadful morons. Over time, through teachings, sermons, and preaching, I was able to convert some of them into real Muslims, to bring them closer to God. I don't take any glory from that. All of it was the work of God.

With Ismaïla, however, it was different. His knowledge of Islam was as striking as the passion that filled him as he recited a verse from the Quran, or an episode of the life of the prophet. He would anticipate my questions, responding with as much detail and accuracy as a devout octogenarian Sufi. In fact, he went even beyond that in his exploration of the impenetrable paths of theosophy. Obviously, his age made the whole thing even more remarkable, and I knew from our first conversation that he was a true Muslim, of the kind I had rarely seen before. To be honest, he reminded me of myself when I was his age. Perhaps he was even more knowledgeable than I was then. And God can bear witness to the fact that I knew quite a lot at the age of eighteen.

We grew closer as the weeks went by. I was cautious to treat him the same way I treated the other men, who would have justifiably been offended had they noticed my preference *for the new member, but I couldn't help it that he was my favorite. And whenever I had the chance, I would pull him aside to exchange a few words on religion. I believe he appreciated those moments. Of all the moments he spent in the camp, these were the only ones during which he could let go without fear of being misunderstood. We spoke a lot. He taught me things, reminded me of others. I introduced him to a different dimension of religion which he didn't know. I don't know which one of us was more enthusiastic about these exchanges . . .*

It feels strange to admit this, but I think that over the last ten years, Ismaïla was my only real friend, the only person with whom I didn't feel obscure and misunderstood.

The others didn't like him very much. While they never admitted it, they viewed his constant meditation, his vague and imprecise gaze which appeared haughty, his tendency toward total isolation and silence, as contempt for them. Evidently, Ismaïla didn't realize this and was under the impression that he was surrounded by brothers who, although perhaps not as knowledgeable about Islam, were nonetheless informed enough to acclaim Allah as the only Savior, to serve him, and to choose Sharia as the only Path.

He was different; different, and therefore strange. Even in my eyes he was an enigma. He was loquacious, voluble, and chatty when it came to talking about Islam, but as soon as the conversation changed to topics of war, strategy, or the taking of Kalep, he would lock himself in hermetic mutism. I was surprised when I caught him inexplicably saddened whenever I spoke to my men about the next attack on Kalep. But the sadness faded quickly, and he remained calm and lost in thought while the others, galvanized, yelled and shouted. One day, more curious than usual, I decided to ask him about his lack of enthusiasm when it came to the siege of Kalep. He answered, looking toward the sky: "I'm not made for war,

Lieutenant. I'm not made for any war, not even the holy war. But I will fight this one, not as a sign of pride but as a duty toward Allah."

It's true, actually, that he was a pitiful warrior.

A few weeks later, most of the Brotherhood's troops joined us. All of the different factions which had been scattered around the desert came together at the gates of Kalep. The garrison tried, unsuccessfully, to organize itself in response to our sudden movements. During those days we were busy assembling the troops, planning the attack with the leaders of the other factions, speaking to our men, teaching them to unite and remain disciplined. At that time, I would only catch brief glimpses of Ismaïla between activities.

I only really saw him again the night before the attack. He was supposed to be part of a group that I had designated to go out and scout as much information as possible on the enemy's troops, without engaging in battle. He left in the morning with the other men in whom I'd placed my confidence. Before his departure, he took me in his arms with affectionate enthusiasm, which was unusual for him, and looked at me, his eyes beaming: "Tomorrow is a big day, Lieutenant: we are finally going home!" At the time I didn't fully grasp the meaning of these words. Today I understand them better. Going home was not simply a metaphor to symbolize the Brotherhood's siege of Kalep; it was the truth. For him, going home meant returning to the land where he was born, where his family lived, and where his past resided. But I hadn't understood. He'd never spoken to me of his past or his family, and I had never asked him. Up until that point, I had strangely believed that because I didn't have one myself, he must also have been alone.

We parted on these words. It was the last time I saw him. He never returned.

In a burst of frenzy, the expeditionary group overstepped

*the boundaries I had set and found themselves in enemy ter-
ritory. My soldiers were attacked by one of the army's battal-
ions. Out of the five men who left, only one of them returned
to me, covered in blood and with a badly wounded abdomen.
Before collapsing in my arms, he told me what happened. He
reported that the group had been very cautious at first, trying
to avoid going past the perimeter that was assigned to them.
But because they could not identify where they were, Ismaïla
himself had convinced them to go further. They argued, but
ultimately moved forward. This decision was a fatal one.
They were attacked and then chased in the desert by an army
vehicle and, after some time, were forced to stand their
ground and take out their firearms. The survivor, who had
been wounded during the first exchanges, returned to the
camp running, and miraculously had not been followed by
anyone from the other side. When I asked him about his com-
rades, he said he didn't know what happened to them, but
that they were probably all dead by now because the soldiers
were greater in number and drove vehicles.*

*Nevertheless, as he was moaning, he was able to describe
to me the last image he had of the battleground: it was of
Ismaïla, weapon in hand, standing vulnerable atop a dune,
opening fire on two soldiers hiding behind the trees, shouting
God's name.*

*And that was it. The soldier died. And with him, surely,
the last image of Ismaïla alive . . .*

*This moved me. I had grown to love this boy over the
course of all these weeks. He, who hated war, had died—
because surely he must have died—fighting it. But he had
loved God and served him up until the very end. That made
him a martyr.*

*That night, I didn't sleep. I prayed for him, for his soul to
be at rest alongside Allah. I went to sleep with a heavy heart,
my mind filled with the image of Ismaïla's eyes staring at me.*

Unfortunately, when dawn came there was no time to be sad or melancholic. It was time to attack. We did, and we were able to take Kalep. Long after, my mind remained with Ismaïla. Only once all my attention turned to the building site of Kalep was I able to start forgetting him a little.

Five years later, I had almost managed to erase Ismaïla's features from my mind. But his eyes . . . I could never forget them. His mother has the same eyes, and that's why I'm startled whenever I see them.

Does she know her son is dead? Did anyone ever tell his family?

I suppose not. And I won't be the one to do it. I have heretics to catch. And besides, what good would it do anyways?

CHAPTER 36

S he opened the door, stunned. He was standing there, motionless; his attitude and posture gave away a sense of discomfort. She was the first to break the silence, once the initial moments of surprise had passed.

"What are you doing here?"

He didn't know what to say.

Madjigueen Ngoné regretted the harsh tone she'd just used. The words had betrayed her and come out on their own. But what else could she have said? Without uttering a word, she looked at Vieux Faye, who was still motionless and awkward. He seemed to be scanning her face for a glimmer of sympathy. Though she tried very hard to remain stoic, even hostile, she felt a sort of warmth rising in her belly. This little game, one of the most beautiful but also tedious aspects of love, lasted some time. The trouble was that neither one of them was truly aware that it was happening. They didn't even know if they were in love and wouldn't dare try to find out. Each of them was repressing what their bodies longed to cry out.

"May I please come in?"

She moved aside, mechanically. Vieux Faye left the little hallway he was standing in and entered the apartment.

It had two rooms and was decorated simply. The main room doubled as a kitchen and living room. To the right was a sofa bed flanked by two burgundy chairs, all of which faced a television resting on a coffee table. Next to the television was a desk that held a shiny computer—undoubtedly the apartment's most luxurious object. Above the desk and attached to the wall was a small shelf with three rows which served as a library and trinket holder: various books mingled with DVDs, little figurines dressed as toreadors in capes and hats stood with exaggerated pride and passion atop boxes and beside scented candles, along with little glass animal statuettes. The rest of the room contained a small wooden table surrounded by three chairs, a stove so clean it seemed to have never been used, and finally a few poufs scattered around randomly. A small door immediately to the left of the entrance led to the bathroom; there was another door in the living room which, Vieux Faye guessed, must lead to Madjigueen Ngoné's bedroom.

"You have a very nice apartment."

"Thank you."

"I hope it's not too expensive. I know the price of real estate is higher here than it is in Soro."

He opened his mouth and then closed it again, almost as if he was about to add something and decided, at the last minute, that it wasn't worth saying. She sat in one of the chairs while he made himself comfortable on the couch. They didn't dare let their eyes meet, and each of them, in heavy silence, pretended to be interested in some random object. The young woman turned the television on and changed channels in search of one that was not mentioning the Brotherhood in some form or another; he stared off at the shelf, trying to read the title of one of the books. The awkwardness lasted for a little while. Then, Madjigueen turned the TV off and headed toward the kitchen.

"What can I get you?"

"Whatever you're having."

A few minutes later, she handed him a cup of tea.

"So, you drink this tea?"

"What do you have against it? It's because it's made with a tea bag, is that it?"

"No . . . no . . . I . . . I just think that ours tastes better, that's all."

"I prefer this one. Also, ours takes too long to brew. This one is more practical."

"I could make you some and change your mind."

As the atmosphere became more relaxed, his confidence grew. Her mask of indifference slowly came off. As beautiful and wild as it made her seem, it also rendered her terribly inaccessible. He liked her better when she was calm, when her lovely eyes were soft instead of harsh. He was happy to see her again.

"You still haven't answered me, Vieux. What are you doing here?"

He looked at her. Her face was no longer stern, but serious, perhaps even a bit sad, as if she was expecting something she feared might never happen. He lowered his eyes and stared at his cup of tea, stirring it gently with a little spoon. He didn't know what to say. Did he even know why he was there? He wanted to get up and leave without saying a word, or disappear, melt into the crevices of the couch he was sitting on. He felt butterflies in his stomach. He was still looking at his tea. But was she still looking at him?

He lifted his eyes. She was shaking, but her gaze was still fixed on him. He lowered his head again, lifted it, lowered it. She was beautiful, dressed simply in a white shirt and distressed jeans. Her hair was pulled back in a tight bun. He could see the outline of her firm breasts rise and fall with the fast pace of her breathing.

He failed to notice that the spoon was shaking, creating a metallic noise as it hit the rim of the glass cup. As soon as he noticed, he let it go. The tea continued to spin, his hand was still shaking.

He was still looking at her. Despite her trembling, she looked like a statue. He opened his mouth, said something, then went quiet.

"I'm sorry? I didn't understand."

"Me neither."

She smiled. That gave him courage. This was the sign he'd been waiting for the whole time.

"I came here because I missed you. I think that's what I said. Because I missed you. I think . . . I think," he continued after a few seconds, "that I was harsh with you last time. I was upset. Forgive me."

"You don't have to apologize for not agreeing with me and expressing that. That's not why I left. I have my beliefs, as we all do, that's all."

"Would you come back to work with us?"

"No, even though I will never really leave you."

"To be honest, I don't really care if you are with us. What I care about is that you are with me. Those meetings were the only times I got to see you. It was good for me. Now that there might not be another one for a long time and that I cannot always come to Kalep, I miss you. I wanted you to know that."

He no longer had trouble finding his words. They were now flowing off of his tongue like running water from a faucet.

"Vieux, why didn't you try to follow me last time? Our goodbye was painful for me . . ."

"I . . ."

He lost his words again.

"I missed you too," the young woman whispered.

She was no longer shaking, but he certainly was, more intensely than ever. She put her cup down and took a seat next to him. He was handsome. She held his arm and laid her head on his shoulder. They stayed like this for a few seconds in silence. He stopped shaking.

"Come . . ."

It wasn't a command, more of a whisper. Not a requirement, but a suggestion, not an overbearing plea but rather a gentle invitation, as if, in her quiet words and their significance, there was something essential to be saved. He stood up. She looked at him, but her face was no longer sad or stern. It didn't give off an air of defiance, the kind which most seductresses give a man at the peak of flirtation to ignite his desire; nor was it awash with the kind of uncontrollable excitement that is often the mark of fiery passion; it was simply calm. He stopped chewing his gum. She had never appeared more beautiful to him than in that instant. He moved closer to her, grabbed her waist without taking his eyes off her. They were so close that each of them could feel the heat of the other's breath. In that moment, their breathing quickened. They closed their eyes together.

When their lips touched for the first time, they forgot everything. The journal. The Brotherhood. The beggars of Kalep. Even the resounding call to prayer felt to them like an ode to their newly born love. And indeed, it was.

They stayed in an embrace for some time before Madjigueen invited Vieux to follow her into her bedroom.

Chapter 37

In Bantika, a city nearly as big and populated as Kalep, there was a library, which was the pride not only of the province, but of all Sumal.

The library had been built after the country acquired its independence, around a time when it was engaged in a vast campaign of national projects to promote the land and its culture. A number of cultural structures were built during this time, which the country continued to showcase to the whole world, almost half a century after their construction. Along with the country's four other libraries, Bantika's national library was a cultural jewel in which Sumal still took tremendous pride. If each of the country's five big libraries was a stone of the country's cultural crown, Bantika's was undoubtedly the most precious—its sparkling gem. The library guarded a secret which granted it notoriety far beyond the borders of the province, the whole country, even the whole continent: the underground room. It was the only library to have one and it gave the city all of its luster. This room housed the country's most beautiful treasure.

What treasure?

Rare documents, historical ones, secular ones written by the elders (who, in the time since their writing, had been elevated to the ranks of founding fathers, and some of them to the ranks of saints), those that told the story of the birth of Sumal, which had previously been the heart of the greatest, most powerful empire of the continent. These documents, as valuable and important as sacred relics, were among the oldest documents that people had used to learn about the continent's history. Some of them were thousands of years old, yet miraculously preserved from the decay of the centuries. They had become treasures—more than treasures, symbols. They had first been discovered some twenty years prior on a research site not too far from the city, by an archeologist and anthropologist whose name was then given to Bantika's university. Their discovery had been a national event that extended to the continent and, eventually, to the entire world. People came from all over to see the evidence that bore witness, not only to the construction of one of the most mythical and powerful empires that the world had ever seen, but to the existence of a genuine culture that was rich, complex, advanced, organized, strong, intelligent, literate, and had existed on this land for centuries. These documents were undeniable proof against the racist and supremacist allegations made by some foreign theorists, who had denied the existence of the continent's advanced civilizations. The documents stored in the library's underground room were not only an extraordinary historical and scientific discovery, they were also an astounding testimony, a birth certificate, a guarantee of identity. They were a way for the continent to assert itself with style and noise in the framework of History. With these documents, the continent could now move past the doorstep of History where, as a well-known philosopher once said, it had long been cooling its heels; it could leave pre-History where, it seemed, it had remained at a standstill. These documents were proof that here too, people had written.

The documents were authenticated and studied, even though rumor had spread that they were fake and that the illustrious scientist who had discovered them had orchestrated a fraud. But reliable scientists conducted tests which were able to dissipate all doubts and confirm the documents' authenticity. The decision was then made to store them in Bantika's library, the cultural flagship of Bandiani (Kalep was more of an economic stronghold), and therefore the rightful guardian of these valuable documents. An underground room equipped with an alarm system was built and the documents—some of them at least, there were many—were stored there. Bantika's library became a pilgrimage site. Lovers of history, philosophy, theology, sociology, mathematics, anthropology of writing, and codicology rushed to see it, crossing paths with tourists from many countries along the way. All of the them reveled in the marvel of these treasures, and the underground room was never empty. First Bantika, then Bandiani, followed by all of Sumal began taking advantage of the newfound notoriety that these documents gave them: tourism grew, infrastructures were built, and Bantika, whose growth was already steady, soared economically. Profits were enormous and every sector of activity reaped the benefits. In the following years, the north of the country became one of the continent's most visited areas.

The final consecration of this sudden popularity happened five years after the documents were discovered, when the international organization for the preservation of world heritage designated Bantika's library—its documents, really: no one cared about the rest—as a world heritage site. What a wonderful and unique privilege to take pride in.

The library in Bantika was, therefore, not merely a library, but a real temple.

And the gods of this temple were on fire that night. In other words, the library was burning.

A sea of people had progressively formed around the city center, where the book burning was taking place. Some had been there since the start of the proceedings, others had run to the scene at the sight of the bright light coming from the square, or as they watched columns of black smoke emerge above the roofs of the houses and rise into the sky, obscuring a clear night.

Abdel Karim had arrived in Bantika just after the evening prayer, leading close to one hundred armed men. He ordered them to break into the library. The alarms had gone off automatically, producing an irritating concert of shrieks which Abdel Karim had managed to quiet down by firing at the devices.

Ever since they had invaded the North, the Brotherhood's fundamentalists had regularly threatened to burn down the library (which the tourists and scientists had deserted since the city was being controlled by the Brotherhood). This threat, while initially only theoretical, was now being enacted through this book burning.

* * *

One must examine in greater detail the potential ideological motivations that pushed the fundamentalists to destroy the library's documents. Their reasons seem to be of three different natures.

The first is practical: the fundamentalists believe these documents to be diabolical instruments because they steal attention away from the Brotherhood. Ideologically, one must understand that for many fundamentalists, the destruction of the Library has little to do with its contents, which they generally don't know much about. What is important is to make room for fundamental ideology, to erase from the public sphere anything which may encourage individuals to stray from the Brotherhood's words. The library must be destroyed not because it carries knowledge that is potentially dangerous to Islam, but rather because this destruction serves as a distraction, a diversion. It's about negating the library as a figure, as a possible physical incarnation of *distraction* (in contrast to the supposed depth of the words of the Brotherhood). From this point of view, most of the fundamentalists see no difference between burning down the library and ransacking a computer room or a nightclub. The fundamentalists destroy the library out of *jealousy*: not because it knows more than they do, but because its presence makes their own invisible.

Hence the second reason, political in nature: to destroy these world-renowned documents is to attract worldwide attention to the Brotherhood, or to remind everyone of the Brotherhood. It's to perpetrate an attack whose victims are symbols rather than men. It's mainly about the desire to be taken seriously, to be considered a full-fledged opponent, to show that they know how to develop a strategy. Simply put, it's about communication.

The third reason is philosophical and literary: it concerns the relationship, conscious or unconscious, acknowledged or denied, obvious or hidden, between ideology (religious and/or political) and writing. In any case, the last reason is the most interesting of the three.

Ideology fears the *writing* of books that it deems dangerous. Of course, this fear comes from the fact that it cannot control their discourse and their contents, two elements which might go against its own interests (by pushing readers toward retaliation, for example); but what it also fears, independently of the consequences these contents may have, is what they imply. The very act of writing is what ideology fears.

Because the act of writing freely is an irrepressible extension of intelligence. To write outside of ideology is to have been the site of an uninterrupted and free expression of intelligence, one which emerges through the very act of writing. Ideology is precisely the negation of this expression of intelligence. In the eyes of ideology, intelligence must either exist within the confined framework that it has established, or must not exist at all (in other words, must be *eliminated*, in every sense of the term). And when ideology burns the books that it deems dangerous, it fears the *idea that they could have been written* outside of ideology in space and time at least as much as it fears their potential outreach. The harmful consequences that the books being erased by ideology could have on their readers are as dangerous as the conditions in which they were written: those of an irrepressible expression of intelligence.

Ideology fears and hates that the writing of dangerous books is the result of a free venture of intelligence; but what ideology *also* wants to burn and negate is the History of free intelligence, and writing is both its signifier and its sign.

* * *

A few onlookers who had seen what was happening told latecomers that half the men were ordered by their captain to empty the library of all its musical documents, because all music was considered diabolical. They also claimed that the humanities and social sciences section had been fully removed, its contents emptied onto the big square in front of the building. All testimonies agreed on the following: Abdel Karim himself had gone to the underground room with a few men, carried out the historical documents, and threw them, without any hesitation, onto the huge stack of books and records that was piling up in front of the library. Then he set fire to it all himself while his men, armed and holding a double security wire around the fire, shouted, giving thanks to God.

The fire rumbled, roared, rattled, exploded, pounced, and greedily swallowed everything it had received as sacrifice with a devastating sensuousness. The flames grew into immense Hydras that projected fantastic and terrifying figures onto the ground. Dark, pungent curtains shrank toward the sky, spun around themselves, and melted everything in their grip. There was something beautiful in all of it, horribly beautiful. The light of the fire cast a glow on people's faces, but also brought out their shadows. Every one of these faces seemed strange and motionless, fascinated by this irrepressible thing that contained both life and destruction. From time to time you could hear the sound of a small explosion amidst the roaring flames: it was some record or glass object making one final groan before becoming one with the whirls of smoke heading for the heavens. The books lying on the edge—the ones which had escaped extermination—were picked up and thrown forcefully into the fire.

Abdel Karim watched the flames, which had begun to slow down, occasionally emitting rebellious flickers which would sparkle vigorously for a few seconds before disappearing entirely.

Nobody had moved. All of the people were still there, as if each of them understood, albeit confusedly, that something fundamental and essential was being lost in this inferno, not only to their city but to their hearts. Something which they were trying to grasp to no avail.

Withdrawn, Abdel Karim closely observed the silhouettes gathered around the fire. He was searching for a sign, a gesture, a suspicious look that might give him some clue as to the identities of the journal's authors. He was certain that by burning the library he would attract those responsible, since these were supposedly cultivated men, who had undoubtedly frequented Bantika's library on multiple occasions. He had written to the authorities to request permission to undertake this book burning, and had argued that it was imperative to act forcefully not only to remind the people of the province that the organization was master of the territory, but also to put them on a path that might lead to the origins of the journal that had defied them. He received their approval swiftly and decided to act immediately, without warning, to have the element of total surprise. Now he was waiting. Watching. Scrutinizing.

No one was moving, for the time being. The fire was slowly dying.

* * *

Déthié and Codou felt defeated. Their silence seemed like mourning. Head between his hands and eyes closed, Déthié looked older, weakened. Codou was standing, leaning against the wall, her head lifted toward the ceiling and her eyes filled with tears. They hadn't exchanged a single word since coming back home. The book burning had robbed them of their desire to speak.

While they had been calmly conversing on their terrace, taking full advantage of the cool evening breeze, they noticed a long trail of dark smoke protruding from somewhere, not too far from the city center. Initially, they thought it must have been a fire, but at no point did they hear shouts or sirens, and so they decided to go and have a look for themselves. On their way, Codou asked a man who had passed them running in the direction of the fire what was happening. The man, breathless, mumbled something which Codou either didn't comprehend or feared she misunderstood: "Abdel Karim and his men . . . fire . . . library . . . supposed to be beautiful." He then disappeared in the maze of the city center's streets.

Once they arrived, she couldn't contain herself and let out a painful cry, a groan, like a beast in agony. Déthié on the other hand remained still, frozen, arms dangling and mouth agape, a look of horror on his face, in a position that gave away how helpless he felt, as he witnessed these books burning. They remained this way, silent like all the others, except their silence was not merely the result of disgust, but also of pain and anger. The two of them had met amongst these books some twenty years prior, and this was also where they had met Malamine. It was thanks to these books that they learned how to be who they had become: it's how Déthié discovered his love of culture and his desire to promote it by becoming a professor; it was also how Codou developed a taste for reading and a desire to convey it to others by becoming a bookseller. Their memories were being scattered by the fire along with the very essence of what they considered to be one of the few true things about man: Knowledge.

Suddenly, Déthié began to tremble with anger. When the fundamentalists began to shout, he'd almost insulted them. If Codou hadn't been there, he would have probably attacked them.

She stopped staring at the ceiling and looked at him. He had not calmed down, but his anger had gone cold.

"How did we get here, Codou? Explain to me how they can make these books pay for the mistakes we made? I accept that I am guilty, as are you, as are the fundamentalists, as is everyone, but why were these books burned? What were they guilty of?"

Déthié's questions were so ridiculous, they expressed such powerlessness, that Codou didn't know how to answer them.

"What did Heinrich Heine say about book burning?" he continued.

"'Wherever books are burned, men in the end will also burn.'" answered Codou faintly.

"I wouldn't wait for these lunatics to burn men. They are already killing many of them more barbarically than any human bonfire. I can't sit here and wait, Codou. I'm going to act, and I'm going to act now."

"What are you going to do?"

"Leave right now and distribute the rest of the copies of the journal that we've been hiding. I won't be able to sleep tonight unless I feel like I've done something to rebel. I have to strike back. Tonight, I will fight."

"I will fight with you. This library they destroyed was the first home to our love, remember?"

"I remember."

He looked at her tenderly.

"This book burning, as horrible as it is, will change things. I feel it, darling. The end of these criminals is near."

"Why do you say that?"

"The West will intervene! As long as only men were dying, they could make do with simply being shaken by the situation and weakly condemning it. But now that books are dead on top of men, now that the very idea of world heritage has been attacked, violated, destroyed, the West can no longer ignore what's happening here. A few men die and it's not the end of the world, we're used to it, but nearly sacred historical documents being burned to the ground, that's even worse. Now we know it, things have changed: when an old man dies, a library doesn't burn to the ground. He is not as valuable."

"What do you mean?"

"That these documents, for some people, have more value than some human lives. Tomorrow you'll see, they'll condemn, threaten, give ultimatums; they'll start a rumor about an imminent intervention; in short, they'll do everything that they haven't done until now, or have only done reluctantly."

"Déthié . . ."

"Yes, I know, perhaps I'm exaggerating a bit. Maybe the pain and anger are overwhelming me and I'm not lucid. What matters is that they intervene, that they help our poor national army to free the North. That's all that counts. That's the only clarity to be had, I think. The end is near, darling. The end is near. But that's not a reason to stop fighting. Let's eat first, then we'll revive *Rambaaj* in memory of Bantika. That name really was an excellent idea, Codou," he ended with a chuckle.

They ate quickly, then Déthié took an old "Abibas" sports bag (a knockoff, obviously) that held the last copies of the journal out from its hiding place in the ceiling. Tomorrow, for the second time in a few weeks, Bantika would wake up to copies scattered around its streets. It would be their response to the book burning. Déthié and Codou kissed before disappearing into the night.

They had only walked a few feet when a dozen armed men surrounded them. Blinded by the strong beam of a flashlight that was pointed at them, they couldn't identify the face of the person who was yelling.

"In the name of Allah, I arrest you in connection to the production and distribution of the journal *Rambaaj*, a collection of godless texts. Do you refuse to identify yourselves as its authors?"

They recognized Abdel Karim's voice. Déthié looked at his wife. She was calm, a smirk graced her lips. One couldn't read any kind of fear on her face. He grabbed her hand and, turning toward the source of the voice, yelled:

"We don't deny it. We are the authors of the journal. Now go burn in hell."

Those were his last words before being knocked down to the ground with the butt of a rifle to his neck. Codou had no time to scream. Another blow to the head and she, too, fell unconscious.

Abdel Karim had prevailed. His plan had worked. Earlier, when the books were burning, he noticed that Déthié could barely contain his nervousness, and his angry gaze could belong only to somebody who opposed the Brotherhood. A few minutes after they'd left, he and a few men had discreetly followed them from a distance. And by early afternoon tomorrow, they would be executed in Kalep in front of the entire province.

CHAPTER 38

By the following morning, the rumor had spread like bushfire around the entire province: Abdel Karim had found the authors of the rebellious journal and would execute them that very afternoon. By ten o'clock, hundreds of people had converged upon the city, some coming out of sheer curiosity, while others, supporters of the Brotherhood, came as if it was their duty to participate symbolically in the execution of those who had become their enemies over the past months. But all of them wished to see what the people who wrote these texts looked like.

The rumor, which was inaccurate but also not entirely false, was first that there were two men, then a man and a woman, and finally three women. Conversations were lively and the excitement was slowly building. The famous square by City Hall was slowly filling up once again, and everyone was trying to secure a good spot to see the condemned.

Malamine was busy with paperwork in his office at the hospital when Alioune entered, a worried look on his face. Malamine could tell something terrible had happened.

"They got Codou and Déthié. I just heard. Apparently last night Abdel Karim burned the books of Bantika's library and shortly after, he caught people with copies of the journal ready to distribute them. They didn't mention Codou or Déthié by name, but they were the only ones who had enough copies left."

"Are you sure of what you're saying, Alioune? Are you really certain?" His heart was pounding.

"I can't be certain, Malamine. I didn't see them. I just know that yesterday, during the night, documents were burned in Bantika's library, including the famous millennial manuscripts of the Bandiani."

"What?"

"Don't you listen to the radio?"

"Not since the Brotherhood took control of it."

"That and the news of the arrest were this morning's main stories."

"We need to calm down, maybe it's not Déthié and Codou. I'm going to try and call them."

"I already tried. They're not answering."

Malamine glanced over at Alioune. A thousand different scenarios were already playing out in his head. He called Déthié immediately. No answer. He left him a few messages and also tried to reach Codou, in vain. Alioune stood in front of him, worried, his hands clenched on the back of a chair. The same questions, hopes, and fears crossed their minds when their eyes met. After multiple unsuccessful attempts, Malamine stood up and tried to collect his thoughts.

"We must stay calm until we're certain that it's really Codou and Déthié. They're not answering but that doesn't necessarily mean they were caught. That rumor could just be a trap to force us to reveal ourselves. We can't give in to panic. First we must warn the others. Is Madjigueen Ngoné here?"

"No. She's off today."

"That's right, I forgot. You must go warn Père Badji. Run to the tavern, fast. In the meantime, I'll call Vieux Faye and Madjigueen Ngoné. No matter what the situation is, we have to talk and think of a solution. The most important thing is to stay calm. We still have a bit of time . . ."

"Not that much time. They say that those who were captured last night in Bantika will be executed this afternoon. Apparently the square in front of City Hall is already filled with people. If there's a decision to be made, we have to make it now, and quickly."

Alioune left. Malamine remained still for a few seconds, his head heavy. In the hallway, the noise of the nurses mingled with the pleas of the sick. He was listening, but his thoughts were meshing and clashing, and he was incapable of focusing on any specific idea. One by one, images of Codou and Déthié, of Abdel Karim, Père Badji, Madjigueen, of Vieux, of Alioune raced through his mind. He opened his eyes and tried to slow his breath. When he lowered his eyelids once again, he could only see his family, whole, with Ismaïla. And everyone was smiling. That image persisted in his mind for a long time, and he would've liked for it to stay forever. He would've liked to stay there, to sleep and wake up only to realize that everything he had learned was just a bad dream. But it was true, it was all true. Alioune went to warn Père Badji, the people were heading to the City Hall square, Déthié and Codou weren't answering, he had to call Madjigueeen Ngoné and Vieux Faye to warn them as well. And, most importantly, his family wasn't whole and not nearly as happy as in his dreams.

He opened his eyes and the daily sounds and commotion assailed him once again. He shook his head, as if to banish his dreams far from his mind, and dialed Vieux's number.

* * *

It was 1:30 P.M. and Malamine still hadn't heard back from anyone. He could reach neither Madjigueen nor Vieux, both of whom had turned their phones off, and Alioune, who had left over an hour earlier to warn Père Badji, still hadn't returned. There was no way to reach him: Alioune, like Père Badji, didn't own a cellphone. Malamine was pacing in his office.

He left when the clock struck 2 P.M., but not before sending a message to Vieux and Madjigueen to say, "Let's meet directly at the City Hall square," and giving instructions to the hospital guard to let Alioune know that he had left. As Malamine was walking away, the guard said, with a silly smile on his face: "Hey doctor, I want to go too! To see our enemies be punished by God. But I can't. You'll let me know how it was, won't you, doctor? They say Abdel Karim will be there and take care of the killing himself!" Malamine didn't answer and continued to head toward the city center. Once he arrived, it was so crowded that they were no longer letting people in. Malamine immediately noticed two stakes about six feet from one another. This sight filled Malamine with fear, and for the first time since Alioune told him about the rumor, he began to actually believe that his friends might be in danger. He froze at this thought. He quickly looked at his phone. Vieux and Madjigueen still hadn't answered him. The crowd was pushing, excited, filled with murmurs; conversations were flowing everywhere you looked, eyes filled with curiosity, people's attitudes either tense or relaxed. Malamine suddenly felt alone amongst the excited breaths and noises all around him. Abundant beads of sweat collected on his forehead.

Malamine was worried. Like all the others, he was waiting.

CHAPTER 39

Ndey Joor Camara, somewhat surprised by the silence in her neighborhood at this hour, turned on the radio and heard the news. She called Malamine immediately.

"Hello? Hello, Malamine . . . ? Yes, no, I can't hear you very well . . . What? Yes, I'm fine, the kids are too . . . Sorry? Try to distance yourself from the noise a bit. There, that's better. Yes, they're O.K. Idrissa is reading in his room and the little one is napping. Malamine, did you hear the news? No, not the shoes . . . The news? About the journal, in Bantika. Apparently they arrested two people. Yes . . . What? You're aware? Oh my goodness, do you know who? You know? No, you don't know . . . You don't know if it's them? It better not be . . . I'm scared, you know. You should stop . . . What? Where are you? City Hall? But what's that noise in the background? What? I'm sorry but I really can't hear you very well . . . An execution? What? Where? Here, in Kalep? Later today? But whose? You don't know whose, yes, you told me . . . But did you reach them? Do you know where they are? Do you know if it's them? You're still not following . . . ? But . . . And the others? Yes I understand, but why didn't you warn me? Please, Malamine, don't do anything that will put you in danger . . . Yes, yes, I understand, but be careful . . . What are you talking about? You're not guilty of anything! They were old enough . . . Malamine, I beg you . . . Listen to me . . . What? Yes, yes, I love you too. Please, please, listen to me . . . You

need to promise me that you won't do anything . . . Promise
me, please. I'm scared . . . Promise . . . Malamine, I . . . What?
Hello? They're coming? Who's coming? Malamine, please,
don't do anything foolish. Think of me and the . . . Hello?
Hello? Malamine? Hello?"

CHAPTER 40

Even though bags were covering their faces, Malamine recognized Déthié and Codou as soon as the militia dragged them out of the vehicle. He recognized Déthié's gait: he walked proudly even though he was being beaten at regular intervals. They'd been allowed to keep their own clothes on, and he recognized Codou's camisole, the one he himself had gifted to her, the one that she loved. It really was them. That sudden certainty made him lightheaded, and he almost fainted. The two shapes creeping forward toward the stakes, followed closely by three armed men, were in fact his friends. And they were the ones who were going to be executed. Behind this little group, Abdel Karim walked slowly, seemingly indifferent to the world around him. As usual, his face was brutish—but strangely enough, he seemed nervous, too. Behind him, roughly one hundred and fifty feet away from the stakes, twelve men were lined up next to a group of around thirty others. There must have been around fifty men in total.

While Codou and Déthié were being tied to the stakes, Malamine was suffocating. He didn't know what to do or what to think. He was expecting his legs to give out at some point. Nobody around him seemed to notice his condition. All of them, holding their breath, were staring at the two bodies whose faces they couldn't wait to see. They whispered: "So it's a man and a woman!" "Poor woman, what is she doing caught up in this?" "Why aren't they naked?" "Are we the ones who are going to do the execution? I don't see stones anywhere," et cetera. Malamine looked again toward the stakes. Déthié and Codou were stoic, there was something majestic and calm about their demeanor.

Abdel Karim's voice brought him back to reality. The giant was standing between the two stakes, holding a megaphone in his hand. Malamine noticed that he looked worn out and tired, probably sleep-deprived. This time, strangely, he didn't feel a sense of hatred like the one that usually overwhelmed him whenever he looked at the giant. Abdel Karim's voice resounded.

"*Audhu billahi mina-Shaitan-nir-Rajeem. Bismilahi rahmani rahim. Assalamu Aleïkum,* my brothers. I thank you again for your overwhelming response to Allah's call. Today is a great day: after all these weeks, the sinners who published the journal that you've been hearing about and who have inflicted chaos on our cities will be punished. They thought they could escape their fate indefinitely. They know now that they might be able to escape men, but never God . . ."

"*Allahu akbar!*" some voices cried out.

"*Allahu akbar,*" my brothers! However, the work here is not done yet. These people did not act alone: I know they had accomplices in the province. They might even be here among us today, at this very moment."

At this moment, there was an uproar from the crowd, and everyone looked over at his neighbor, as if meaning to say "it's not me" and "maybe it's you." This chaos lasted a few minutes. Malamine struggled to appear indifferent, but he had the feeling that every time someone looked over at him, his cover was blown. He kept his eyes fixed on Déthié and Codou. The latter, who had lowered her head to her chest, seemed exhausted. He almost jumped out of the crowd a couple of times in order to try and do something. But what?

Abdel Karim continued.

"These sinners didn't speak despite our questioning, which

lasted all night. They were silent, didn't say a word. I must admit that their stubbornness is somehow admirable. But it's useless. Whether they denounce their friends or not, they will die, and we will find the others just as we found them, God willing. Nothing will stop us on our path toward the truth. Nothing. *Allahu akbar!*"

A few soldiers chanted the name of God, but Malamine noticed that the people were suspiciously silent. Only a few timid sounds escaped from the crowd, which quickly fell silent again, as if overcome by passivity. It was the first time that this crowd didn't seem completely transfixed by Abdel Karim's orations. He wondered if maybe the crowd's grim self-restraint was inspired by the guilty couple's resistance to the Brotherhood.

Abdel Karim took a few steps back and gestured to the line of twelve men about thirty feet away. They loaded their weapons and aimed. Silence overcame the crowd. Malamine was shaking, his eyes filling with tears which he forced himself to wipe away to avoid attracting any attention. He felt like a coward, and this feeling overwhelmed him. At that moment, he thought he would kill himself for letting his friends die. They remained extraordinarily stoic. Malamine thought of their faces. That was probably too much for him to bear: he wavered and nearly fell. He was caught from behind and placed back on his feet, as if they wanted to force him to watch his friends' death up until the very end. Tears were now streaming down his cheeks for all to see; he was no longer trying to hide them. What for? Whether he was caught or someone gave him away didn't matter anymore. At this moment he felt as if he was regaining strength, or rather as if all weakness was leaving his body. He would watch.

That was true surrender. The ultimate display of weakness. He watched nonetheless.

Abdel Karim stared at the motionless crowd. The silence

was unbearable enough to kill someone with a weak heart. The giant was still waiting. His men were standing by for his order to fire, but he wasn't moving, as if attempting to push the potential accomplices, likely standing in the crowd, to the very brink.

"Fire, in the name of God!" Déthié's voice burst forth, defying the entire crowd, the soldiers, the people, Abdel Karim, the silence, and even God.

"Are those your last words, infidel?" the giant shouted.

"No. I'd like to say one last thing to my friends, I know they are there, that they're watching, that they're listening, and that they're hurting. I would like to tell them to continue to fight, to keep going for us, my wife and myself. Do not let our death add any more to your suffering. The battle must continue, my friends."

He stopped talking. Once again, the crowd moved about. Malamine was still. He felt empty and exhausted. He only wanted one thing: for all of this to be over.

"Your sliver of bravery is useless, infidel: we'll find your friends and we'll put them through the same fate as you and your wife. Now," he added turning toward the crowd, "I'm giving the accomplices one last chance to come forward, if they're here and have a minimum of honor and courage. Show yourselves!"

Nobody moved.

A beastly smile drew across the giant's lips. He began to raise his hand slowly toward the firing squad. Twelve rifles were waiting.

"Fire!" he shouted.

A loud bang resounded and one of the twelve men standing in the middle of the line collapsed with a moan.

"That one's for my dog."

People turned around toward the spot where the voice and bullet seemed to have originated from. Père Badji, standing a few feet in front of the crowd, had already reloaded his rifle and was aiming at the row of soldiers again. The sun's rays reflected along the weapon's barrel, which the old man was clenching against his shoulder. He was backlit: Malamine could only see his silhouette cutting through the intense light. Like the others, he was so shocked that no sound could escape his mouth. Abdel Karim himself seemed petrified.

"Père Badji, is that you? No!" yelled Déthié.

Père Badji reloaded his weapon. His gestures were quick, precise. He fired a second shot. Another soldier fell without a cry. All of this had happened very quickly.

"And that," continued Père Badji even though his second victim was already drowning in his own blood, "that one's for . . ."

No one would ever know who that second bullet was for: in a mechanical roar, the soldiers opened fire on Père Badji: fifteen, twenty, thirty bullets pierced his body, and he fell backwards into the dust. The other bullets that missed hit other people in the crowd. Five or six bodies fell, including a young child standing in the front row.

Shrieks of horror overtook the square.

It was a stampede. Cries erupted from everywhere. Men, women, and children were shouting; everyone running around, lost, in search of cover. Dust rose as a result of all the commotion and movement. All anyone could hear were shrieks and profanities. Malamine had been knocked over; he was on the ground trying to stand but his legs stopped him. He saw bodies falling, tripping, colliding. After a few seconds of this utter and indescribable chaos, he heard two shots, followed by Abdel Karim's terrible voice which dominated all of the surrounding noise.

"Fire, fire in there! The accomplices are there! Fire!" he yelled.

Malamine suddenly heard other shots being fired and cries

of pain. He managed to stand again and noticed that civilians were fighting against soldiers. He saw an elderly woman receive a bullet right in the head and fall like an old piece of dead wood, eyes wide open, before noticing that the soldier who had just shot her was hit in the head with a huge brick by an angry civilian standing behind him.

Cries and insults mixed with the sounds of the soldiers trying to reload their weapons. Malamine, who didn't realize his head was bleeding, ran toward the place where the violence seemed most intense. Before joining the mob, he lifted his eyes and noticed a cloud of stones flying toward what looked like a small group of soldiers. He recognized Vieux Faye's voice yelling, "Careful! Behind you, Madjigueen." Without trying to figure out where the voice was coming from, he ran straight into the fight. He saw two bodies intertwined in the dust, beating each other. One of the men, a soldier, was stretched out on his back and, on top of him, the other man was punching him furiously in the face. Malamine was on his way to help him when, suddenly, the man who seemed to be in the lead collapsed: his opponent had shoved a knife in his side and the poor man was now bleeding to death, his body twitching and shaking abruptly. Malamine thought he recognized Birame Penda, the city's most well-known beggar, who was always singing. He didn't have time to verify this identity, as the soldier threw himself at Malamine, his face dripping with blood. He couldn't push him back and both of them began rolling in the dust. Malamine stood up and before his opponent could do the same, he kneed him in the chin, knocking him back down. Malamine was about to throw himself on his opponent's body in order to secure victory when a hand held him back. He turned around.

"Alioune . . ."

"I'll take care of him. Go look for Déthié and Codou. The people are with us. The fighting has spread all over the city.

Père Badji's body was taken to a safe location, I took care of it. Vieux and Madjigueen joined us."

"Yes, I know . . . We must . . ."

The young nurse was no longer listening and already throwing himself on Malamine's assailant who, despite his dreadful state, began picking himself back up. Malamine forgot what he was about to say, turned around, and ran. While gunshots were becoming less and less frequent, cries still resounded in the square. In his race toward the stakes, Malamine saw a group of civilians surrounding two soldiers who had lost their weapons. Behind him he heard their screams. He could no longer hear Abdel Karim's voice. Was he dead? Had he escaped? Was he still fighting and killing? And Déthié? And Codou? He hoped with all of his heart that they were still alive and that, in the midst of all the chaos, people had forgotten they were there.

He got to the place where his friends had been tied up. Both bodies were sagging. They were dead. Déthié had a bullet in his chest. Codou had been hit in the head, and the bag covering it was drenched in blood.

Malamine fell to his knees and screamed.

"It was you! I knew it was you! I will kill you just like I killed them."

Malamine turned around and saw Abdel Karim. The giant's right leg was bleeding from a horrible wound probably caused by the blade of a sharp knife. His sweaty arms were covered in sand and his chest under his open vest offered a glance at his muscular body, a sign of his herculean strength. He was coming forward toward him, limping, pointing a gun at him. Malamine looked at him without saying a word. He was scared.

"You're going to die. You're all going to die."

"No, wait, Captain! I beg you!"

It wasn't Malamine who spoke but Ndey Joor, who came running, covered in sand and with her hair undone. She was barefoot.

She stood between her husband and the colossus who hadn't moved. His arm was extended mechanically, still holding the gun pointed toward the couple. His eyes were demonic.

"I beg you, Captain. I implore, don't shoot."

"Adjaratou, get out of here. Your husband is a traitor and an infidel. God orders me to kill him," Abdel Karim managed to say, even if Ndey Joor's sudden appearance had shaken him.

"Does God only order you to kill, Captain? Which God is that?" she pleaded.

"Mine. And yours. Now move!"

"I beg you . . . Don't do this."

Malamine, as if a stranger to the scene, couldn't move. He saw his wife from behind and noticed the big scars underneath her transparent boubou.

"Adja, this is the last time I'm going to say this, move!"

"Then kill me with him."

The giant was speechless. The woman had uttered these words so calmly that he wondered if she even feared death. He stared at her. He saw Ismaïla's eyes, his face, his smile.

"Ismaïla had the same eyes as you . . ."

"What? You said Ismaïla . . . You know him?"

"I knew him . . ."

A bang resounded. Abdel Karim, whose hand was still holding the gun pointed at Ndey Joor and Malamine, convulsed. When his body shuddered as a result of the impact, he accidentally pulled the trigger; the weapon had fired and then fell abruptly, like a stone, onto the sand. The captain fell to his knees and appeared to choke. His lifeless eyes became cloudy.

"*Allahu Akbar*," he whispered. He found the strength to smile one last time. The smile was peaceful, human, serene.

A second bullet hit him in the head. He crumpled forward, his large body falling heavily on the ground. His brains mingled with the sand.

Behind the dead captain, Malamine saw his son, Idrissa. He

was the one who had shot Abdel Karim. He was holding Père Badji's old rifle. He was still shaking, his hands clutching the weapon.

"Mama," the young man sobbed . . .

Malamine lowered his eyes. His wife was lying at his feet, her eyes closed. A large stain of blood was visible on her stomach. Abdel Karim Konaté's last involuntary shot had hit her.

From afar, the clamor of the fighting was beginning to die down . . .

CHAPTER 41

D*ear Aïssata,*

Can I be frank? I told you that these people would be unpredictable until the end. And here's your proof. Not to say that I trust them. They have bursts of courage, of madness, of cowardice; nobody knows what's going to hit them next. But today, they decided to rebel and to fight.

The news of the fight made its way to Bantika almost instantly. My neighbor ran over and shouted, "They're fighting! They're fighting in Kalep!" And immediately I thought of you. I can't imagine you being amidst this chaos, the bleeding, the violence. Those people don't know what it really means to fight; us, we know it better than anybody.

I hear that Abdel Karim is dead. The rumor of his death spread here, too. The Brotherhood's troops retreated back into the desert, and now the city is empty. Strangely, even though there are no more jihadists strolling through the streets with their weapons, Bantika remains silent and sad. People go out, walk like shadows, surprised by their newfound freedom and clueless as to what to do with it, as if they had completely forgotten what it was like to feel free. They smile awkwardly, it's sad.

People say that it's not over, that the Brotherhood hasn't really left the province, only retreated temporarily into the desert in order to better seize the city. They claim they went to get backup. I believe them. I think they will come back quickly and that they will seize the cities again. They will be better armed than before, more brutal, more barbaric. They will think that their defeat was a sign from God, a test to warn them. And so, to redeem themselves, they will be more violent, more vicious. But they know now. They know that, in the span of a bloody afternoon, those people they thought of as sheep can become wolves. After Kalep's revolt, nothing will ever be the same as before. Nothing. They can keep torturing, beating, executing, but something will have changed. Some people here are prepared to rebel. They brandish the journal and read excerpts. Bravery is being reborn. They had forgotten the taste of freedom, but they now know that it's worth fighting for. I knew the man and the woman, the authors of the journal, they died during the fights. The man used to be my son's professor at the university and the woman owned a bookstore here where Lamine would go often when he was a child. He liked to read. They were neither gods nor heroes, but simple people who could no longer bear the situation. We must be like them.

Resistance is growing here, Aïssata. We are waiting for the return of the bearded men. This time, I will fight. Not to be a hero, but so that my son will not have died in vain. It's time for me to join this fight. I feel strong enough now. Mourning killed me. It's time for me to be reborn. A few weeks ago, I wanted to die; that's no longer the case. Now, I want to live, live with all my strength. I am preparing myself. My husband ended up following the Islamists into the desert, leaving us here, the other wives and myself. When he returns, he will officially be on the other side. We will be enemies. I am ready to kill him with my bare hands. After mourning my son, Aïssata, I want to avenge him. It's my turn to tell you that we must be strong.

A different battle is on the horizon. I hope you will be a part of it, my friend.

Sadobo

CHAPTER 42

Dear Sadobo,

I don't understand what you're saying. I don't know what's gotten into you. All of a sudden, you're strong? In my case, mourning made me understand that it's impossible to be strong after all we've been through. You want to fight for your son so that he won't have died in vain? But he did die in vain. He died for nothing. He died absurdly. Like my daughter. Nothing will bring them back. Not the blood that you'll shed, not the tears. You're right, even if you seem to have forgotten: what's the point of trying to be strong? My child's death will be my eternal weakness. I won't stand up again. I no longer want to.

I was at home during the battle. My husband had gone out. He came back with a broken arm. I was completely indifferent. And I'm not a monster, I love him. But the suffering of others seems so irrelevant in comparison to my own that it no longer moves me.

I heard the cries, the gunshots, the screaming, and all of it seemed foreign, insignificant. Some fights even happened right under my window. I saw a group of civilians throw themselves on a soldier and beat him to death. Who will ever be able to explain such an act to me? And what could even explain it? Anger? Vengeance? Hatred? For a few moments, I saw them all, drowning in the most all-consuming violence.

Do you remember my neighbor, Ndey Joor, the one who

was beaten? She was wounded by a bullet during the fight-
ing. She died this morning. She clung to life for a few days but
ended up letting go, surrounded by her son, daughter, and
husband. It pained me to hear the news because I liked her. I
will go to her funeral. What's stupid about war is how indif-
ferent it is to people, to their qualities, to their stories: every-
one can die. It's arbitrary. You want to fight? I won't stop
you. The day that you stop writing to me, I'll know you're
dead. Fight if you so wish. I'm completely indifferent. My
daughter is dead. That's the only thing I care about.

You're optimistic. But nothing will change. This rebellion
was an inexplicable happenstance. When the Brotherhood
come back—because they will come back—nobody will
remember the revolt. They will take back the city without
any trouble. And everything will start all over again. Like
before. Others will die absurdly. I don't even hope for hope
anymore, Sabdobo. It's over.

From now on, I will go to the cemetery every day to visit
my daughter's grave. The sign is still there. I will pray for you.
Be careful. I love you.

Aïssata

EPILOGUE

One week after the rebellion in Kalep, the city quickly fell back under Islamist control. The Brotherhood returned in force, led by a new police chief. As a warning, he executed ten random civilians on the very day of his arrival. The deceased captain Abdel Karim Konaté was celebrated as a martyr and cited as an example to follow. A beautiful tomb mounted on a polished marble platform was erected for him in the center of Kalep.

Around the same time, the government issued a statement announcing a new, imminent military operation to free the North. The statement mentioned that the admirable bravery of the people of Kalep, many of whom were killed or wounded during the fighting, had deeply moved the international community. Outraged by the Islamists' barbaric behavior and revolted by the destruction of the manuscripts of Bantika's library—considered world heritage—the international community decided to organize a military effort to help the country's army, which, by then, had been further weakened.

Of course, the statement didn't mention when this effort would take place, and it appears that no official estimate was given.

ACKNOWLEDGMENTS

I'd like to extend my utmost gratitude to all of my friends and mentors who so graciously read, reread, encouraged, critiqued, commented on, and provided inspiration for this novel.

I value their friendships too much to reveal their names. But it is my hope that they will recognize themselves.

I'd also like to thank the entire team at Présence Africaine Editions for their unwavering trust and support.